BADGE OF DISHONOUR

When the US marshal chasing him dies accidentally, outlaw Barton Clancy rides the marshal's horse into Tularosa to rejoin the Paltroe brothers' gang. But he finds Hank Paltroe is waiting to be hanged. Now the town is in fear that the other brother, Josie, will attempt to rescue him. Mistaken for the dead US marshal, Clancy is welcomed as Tularosa's saviour. Then, involved with a local girl, he has to decide whether his loyalty lies with the townsfolk or the outlaws. But has he made the right choice?

TERRY MURPHY

◆

BADGE OF DISHONOUR

Complete and Unabridged

LINFORD
Leicester

First published in Great Britain in 2004 by
Robert Hale Limited
London

First Linford Edition
published 2005
by arrangement with
Robert Hale Limited
London

British Library CIP Data

Murphy, Terry
    Badge of dishonour.—Large print ed.—
Linford western library
    1. Western stories
    2. Large type books
    I. Title
    823.9′14 [F]

    ISBN 1–84617–015–X

Published by
F. A. Thorpe (Publishing)
Anstey, Leicestershire

Set by Words & Graphics Ltd.
Anstey, Leicestershire
Printed and bound in Great Britain by
T. J. International Ltd., Padstow, Cornwall

This book is printed on acid-free paper

1

It was an hour before dawn, when the moon was down, but the sun not yet up. With the first streaks of red beginning to fleck the sky, Barton Clancy rode fast out of the foothills and reined up. Rising up in the stirrups, he scanned the terrain. Ahead of him was a vast, brown, open space. Close behind him was the US marshal who had been relentlessly on his tail ever since the failed bank raid in Raimondo. That was close to two weeks ago, and Clancy had neither rested nor eaten properly in that time. To ride on out into the open now would make Clancy an easy target for a pursuer who had proved himself to be a highly skilled man-hunter. Neither was turning back an option: to do that would give the lawman every advantage.

Born in an outlaw camp, Clancy had cut his teeth gnawing on the barrel of a

Navy Colt and had matured into a feared fast-gun, but the marshal following him held all the aces in this game. Only a fool went up against a stacked deck. Clancy had glimpsed the lawman only once. He was a grey-haired man dressed in dark-grey garb. Even the complexion of his hard face seemed grey. The eyes that had stared momentarily back at Clancy had a coldness that had sent a shiver down his spine.

With no alternative, Clancy spurred his sweating, exhausted horse and rode out into the open. Now he had two choices: he could keep to a fast canter, sparing his horse, reserving whatever energy remained in the hard-ridden animal for a last dash for cover far up ahead, or he could push the horse to the limit at the start to put distance between himself and the marshal, regardless of the consequence. Glancing over his shoulder, he saw the marshal come riding out of the foothills. It was a sight that made up Clancy's mind for him. Hitting the horse's flanks hard with the spurs, he sent it off at a fast gallop, its mane and tail flying in the wind.

The gallop slowed within minutes. Aware that the horse would never make it across the seemingly unending stretch of open land, Clancy knew that his only chance was to pull his rifle from the saddle scabbard, dismount and lie flat for a shoot-out with the lawman. It wasn't much of a chance. The astute marshal would see what he was up to, and would have the opportunity to cut Clancy down before his left foot had cleared the stirrup.

Even so, there was nothing else that Clancy could do. He had his hand on the stock of his rifle when he felt the horse falter under him. Though never a man to panic, Clancy feared the worst. But relief swept through him as his horse picked up its laboured pace again. But it was only a brief respite. First dropping its head, the horse went down in a rolling collapse that sent Clancy flying forwards. He hit the hard ground with an impact that knocked the breath out of him.

Recovering quickly, seeing the bloody foam bubbling round its open mouth, its eyes rolling wildly, Clancy knew that his horse had been shot. Using his elbows, he scrambled on his stomach toward the dying horse. Intending to use it as a shield while he fired at the approaching marshal, he cursed his luck when he saw that the horse had fallen with the rifle trapped under it.

Drawing his six-shooter from its holster, he was aware that it would be useful only if the lawman was foolish enough to come in close. That wouldn't happen. Clancy knew that the marshal was anything but stupid. Raising his head slowly and carefully to look up over the body of the horse, Clancy saw the lawman coming ahead at a canter, his rifle cradled in his arms across his chest. There was a self-assured determination in the marshal's unhurried advance. A veteran lawman, he was confident that he had his man, that the end of the chase was nigh.

Even with the horse for protection, Clancy had no doubt that the mounted marshal would be able to get him with a shot from his rifle long before he came within range of a hand gun. Accepting that this was the end, Clancy decided that he would make it a grandstand finish, just like the admirable last stand made by 'Young' Tyler when he knew that the game was up at Raimondo. With two members of the Paltroe gang lying dead in the dust of the street, the wild and handsome Tyler, his horse having been shot from under him, had walked down the street towards the sheriff's men, his gun blazing.

On that fateful day when they had ridden into town unaware that the law was lying in wait, 'Young' Tyler had died the death of a hero, and two more of the gang had been blasted without knowing what had hit them. The Paltroe brothers, Josie, the tough and resourceful leader of the gang, and the fearless Hank, had escaped. Riding hard out of town, they had taken the rest of the gang with them, except for Clancy. A hail of lead from riflemen up on the flat roof of a tailor's shop had separated him from the others. Lying low until darkness had fallen, he had managed to sneak quietly from the town. Less than an hour later he learned that the US marshal was tailing him.

Now it was all over. Caught in the open, he was about to be gunned down. Probably a fitting finish to a doomed bank raid that hadn't yielded as much as a cent, Clancy thought wryly. Then, unable to believe his eyes, he stood up to make sure that what he had seen had really happened. Life had never done him any favours, until now. The marshal's horse had stepped in a hole and turned a somersault, throwing its rider.

The horse was up on all fours again, prancing around, shaking its head like crazy. But the marshal lay inert on the dull-brown ground. Colt held at the ready, Clancy advanced cautiously to where the lawman was lying, still unmoving. Reaching the marshal, Clancy kept him covered as he dropped to one knee. The man's half-lidded eyes appeared to have the opaque stare of the dead, but a puzzled Clancy couldn't see a mark on him. Reaching out to hold the marshal's square chin between a thumb and forefinger, Clancy moved the head for a better look. But the head fell loosely to the side as if no longer attached to the body. The fall had broken the lawman's neck.

Standing upright, Clancy went up warily to the marshal's horse. It was a dark dun with fiery eyes, a black stripe down the centre of its back, and curious markings on the hocks. As Clancy neared, it arched its back like a cat about to fight. Moving slowly, dreading that the horse might bolt to leave him afoot in the wilderness, he stretched out a hand to grasp the reins. Murmuring softly he gently touched the horse. Now it was just a matter of mounting up and he would be away.

But Clancy's conscience stayed him. Turning his head he looked down at the body of the marshal. The lawman had intended to take away either his liberty or his life. But although the dead have no rights, no man deserved to be left for the buzzards and coyotes to tear to pieces. Securing the horse's reins to a large stone, Clancy walked around, stamping to test the hardness of the ground. By this time the ascending sun had gathered strength to bring out a keen acrid smell from the earth. Choosing a soft spot, he used his heels and his hands to fashion a shallow grave. Rolling the marshal's body into the small hollow, he covered it by making a mound out of the largest stones he could find.

Stepping back from the makeshift grave, he bowed his head for a moment out of respect for a worthy adversary. Then, satisfied that he had afforded the lawman as much dignity as circumstances would allow, he went back to the horse. The animal sat back, snorting wildly. Then the frightened beast charged at him without warning. But Clancy was quicker. Diving under the belly, he took the horse by surprise by mounting from the offside. Still unnerved by the tumble it had taken, the horse bucked and plunged. Putting up its back it arched its neck, playing with the bit, the inside rollers of which jingled against its teeth.

Then Clancy had the horse under control. Settling in the saddle, he rode steadily west. For the first time in almost two weeks he was not a hunted man with the law trailing him. With the horse at a walking pace and the warmth of a rising sun on his back, he enjoyed an intoxicating feeling of freedom.

He headed for Tularosa. There he could rejoin Josie Paltroe, who would have already begun the preliminaries to rob the bank there.

Clancy had ridden into the head of Santa Rosita Canyon and had travelled the canyon trail for a half-mile when he caught the tangy smell of smoke in the air. The trail here traversed a narrow vega, and on the thick grass the hoofs of his horse made no sound. Ahead was a rocky point about which the trail bent. Halfway to this point was a screen of cottonwoods and willows.

A light wagon stood with its shafts resting on the ground, while a thick-limbed horse grazed peacefully nearby. Clancy's every sense was instinctively keyed to tautness. Catching the smell of coffee and bacon frying made him feel ravenously hungry. Smoke rose from a fire at which the solitary figure of a man squatted with his back to Clancy, who relaxed instantly and urged his horse forward at a walk.

The man didn't turn so much as his head as Clancy rode up slowly. That was strange in a land where survival demanded that a man be alert at all times. Pulling the marshal's horse to a stop, Clancy spoke without dismounting.

'It don't pay to let a man ride up on you, mister.'

Remaining in a hunkered position, the man at the fire moved nothing but his slightly hunched shoulders in a shrug. He spoke with an accent that was alien to Clancy. 'I heard you coming, sir. Had you decided to shoot me from afar, then that would be my fate and there was no way that I could alter it.'

'I reckon that's true enough. mister,' Clancy agreed. The aroma from the pan the man was holding over the fire was overwhelming. 'But you'd sure have been wise to be ready to defend yourself when I rode in closer.'

This time the man gave a shake of his head. 'I am not a fighting man, sir. Had you wished to kill me, then I see that as a failing on your part rather than something lacking in myself. Would you care to alight, sir, and join me at breakfast?'

'That's mighty kind of you, mister,' Clancy said, dismounting. 'You sure

have a funny way of looking at things'
— Clancy closed his eyes and slowly
breathed in the aroma of meat frying
— 'but I'd say you're a great cook.'

'I do my best.' The man at the fire
turned to Clancy for the first time. He
was young but with a strangely old face.
His chin was prominent, and his wide,
thin-lipped mouth was set in the
studious expression of a scholar dedicated to learning. It was the face of a
man who constantly questioned everything in life. The eyes that steadily met
Clancy's, slanted upwards at the outer
corners, putting Clancy in mind of a
wolf. Yet there was nothing fierce about
the man, who had an innate gentleness
about him.

'I guess you're not from around these
parts,' Clancy said, as he accepted
gratefully the tin mug of coffee he was
passed. He, too, hunkered beside the
fire.

'I hail from New York, sir.'

A surprised Clancy remarked, 'You're
a long way from home, mister. Would it

be real impolite of me to ask what brings you out here and where you're heading?'

'Not at all,' the man responded. Clancy's thinly veiled question made the corners of his wide mouth flicker in the hint of a smile. 'I am a craftsman, sir, and it is my work that brings me into this wild land that the Almighty seems to have forsaken.'

Eyes devouring in advance the fried food the man was heaping on a plate for him, Clancy put out his right hand. 'The name's Barton Clancy, mister.'

'I'm pleased to meet you,' the man said, putting down a cooking utensil to take Clancy's hand. 'Most folk call me Gilbert.'

'That'll do me, Gilbert, names aren't important out here,' Clancy acknowledged, as he wolfed food, swilling it down with regular mouthfuls of coffee.

'You may consider this to be a somewhat odd question, Mr Clancy, but do you have a hero? Someone past or present whom you look up to?'

'Young' Tyler, going out in glory with his six-gun blazing, sprang to Clancy's mind as he chewed happily. But he guessed that Tyler wasn't quite what the peculiar Gilbert had in mind. So he replied, 'Can't say that I have, Gilbert.'

'Many years ago I read the book Jack Ketch wrote of his life, and I have been captivated by the man ever since that time. Are you familiar with the man and his work, Mr Clancy?'

'Can't say that I am, Gilbert.'

Leaning forward, Gilbert looked intensely, a brightness in his odd-shaped eyes, at the still eating Clancy. 'Jack Ketch was the renowned high-executioner of Great Britain, Mr Clancy.'

'Hold it there a dang minute.' Clancy stopped chewing and gulped down the food in his mouth. 'Are you telling me that you are a hangman?'

'I'm telling you that I am a perfectionist, Mr Clancy,' Gilbert answered. 'I perform a valuable service not only to the community, but to the condemned persons themselves.'

'I reckon as how they wouldn't agree with you, Gilbert.'

'On the contrary. The dispatching of the doomed by the old 'trap gallows' system was barbaric, Mr Clancy. I remember reading of the horrifying execution of Angelo Cornetti, and that decided me to act. As a butcher I regularly visited the slaughterhouse, and the hoisting of the cattle there intrigued me. Studying that made me apply the principle of the windlass to perfect an apparatus for the humane accommodation of the law-breaking community. I boast not, Mr Clancy, when I say that I am an artist with such a fine sympathy as to inspire confidence even in the victim himself at the final hour. You have probably heard of me, sir. I was called upon to act as executioner of Captain Beale, on Governors Island, and of Captain Kennedy at Fort Lafayette.'

The two names had a vague familiarity but held no significance for Clancy.

Rolling a cigarette, he slid a knife from its sheath. Probing the fire with the knife, he speared a bit of burning wood on the point and lit his cigarette. 'Sorry, Gilbert, but I can't say that I've ever heard of you. What brings you way out to these parts?'

'These days my services are in demand all over the United States. I was not far from here when I was asked to do a little job in the town of Tularosa. I shall be on my way there once I have finished my meal.'

'They got a hanging in Tularosa, have they?' In Clancy's business it was bad news to learn of a hanging. It was likely to be someone he knew who was going to the gallows, and one day it could well be him. Draining his mug, he stood up and passed it to Gilbert. 'Thank you kindly for the meal, Gilbert, it was right Christian of you. Now I'd best be riding on.'

Gilbert got to his feet. He was a little bent over when standing, his shoulders held high, his neck so short that it was virtually non-existent. 'Should you also be travelling to Tularosa, Mr Clancy, might I suggest that we travel the road together? I would welcome the company. Loneliness comes with the job, much to my regret.'

'I kinda like you, Gilbert, and I'd sure like to get to know you some more on the ride into town,' Clancy explained. 'The problem is the difference in the way you and me make a living. There's a likelihood that one day I'll be meeting you in your professional capacity, and that would be real embarrassing for both of us.'

Studying Clancy closely, brow furrowed, Gilbert gave a curt nod of understanding. 'Then our parting now has to be yet another of life's many regrets, Mr Clancy. The short time we have spent together has been most pleasurable.' He tentatively held out his hand. 'Might I wish you God speed. I pray that we shall meet again, but not under the dismal circumstances that you predict.'

'*Hasta la vista*,' Clancy said as he took the proffered hand.

As he rode away a sudden and sobering thought hit him. He, Barton Clancy, had just shaken hands with a hangman!

⋆　⋆　⋆

Judge Michael Keily stood in a wide-legged stance in the entrance to Tularosa. He was a tall man with a deceptively gangling body. He had been standing in the centre of the dusty street for two full days and most of two nights, ever since Abel Turner, the town marshal had been shot dead. The desperado who had killed Abel was locked in the town's jail. Having been tried and found guilty, the condemned man had a date with death as soon as the executioner arrived in town. Having been warned that the prisoner had been one of a gang of outlaws who were certain to attempt to rescue him, Keily had set himself up to check out everyone riding into town.

Those who had reason to dislike the arrogant judge were muttering in the town's saloons that the dark-faced, heavily jowled Keily was a symbol of law and order rather than an effective guardian of the town. But most Tularosa folk knew differently. In his tall top hat, high-collared shirt, and long-tailed coat, the judge was something of a ludicrous figure. But when he was roused, something separate took over his body, using it with remarkable speed and enormous strength. He had been witnessed beating hard men who were half his age to a pulp in fair fights. Nobody had ever seen him draw the ivory-handled, long-barrelled Frontier Colt that he wore high round his waist, but the wise people of the town thought it possible that he could handle the gun with the same lightning deftness that he used his fists.

At his side now was Deputy Town Marshal Tommy Oakes, a man in his early twenties, a self-proclaimed hard

19

man who talked tough. Oakes held a scattergun at an angle in the crook of one elbow. His black Stetson was pushed back so that a mop of curly yellow hair was on show; the impressionable young girls of the town regarded him as incredibly handsome. But their elders were better judges of men. They could detect the pattern of degeneracy underlying the boy's fresh good looks, and were wary of him.

Behind the two men an oppressive quietness hugged the broad and dusty street. There were a few horses at the long hitching racks fronting the Majestic Saloon and Texas Jack McNeil's bar, but an unusual silence gripped the whole town. Everyone was fully aware of just how dangerous was the man held in the town's jail. Tularosa had always been a peaceful place to live, with only the high spirits of drunken cowboys occasionally and relatively harmlessly disturbing that peace.

Furthermore, most everyone dreaded the prospect of an imminent hanging in their town. Agreeing that the killer of Abe Turner deserved to be put to death, most Tularosa folk heartily wished that the execution could be carried out elsewhere. The further away from Tularosa the better.

A girl came out of the Majestic Saloon. She started in their direction, and a shaggy yellow cur that lay stretched at full length in the damp shadow of an old log water trough, got unsteadily to its feet to walk listlessly behind her.

'Here comes Cora with a bottle of lemonade for you, Oakes,' the judge commented as the saloon girl came nearer. 'Watch yourself, son. That gal has a knowing look in her eye when she's around you. When a woman has a knowing look in her eye it means that it's time to run.'

'I don't want to do no running, Judge,' Oakes said sulkily. 'Cora's real special. We've got plans, Judge. She wants a proper wedding, sweetpeas and all them kind of things.'

Clicking his tongue in disgust, Judge

Keily said scornfully, 'Didn't your mammy never tell you that saloon gals ain't for marrying?'

'Cora ain't no ordinary girl,' the deputy protested angrily.

The girl came up to them, her moccasined feet moving silently on the dusty street. Loosely arranged as always, her hair flamed over her shoulders as she passed through arrows of sunlight. She was wearing a dark-blue dress, simply cut. Her eyes flirted with Oakes as she held out a bottle to him.

'Here you are, Tommy. You must be thirsty.' She handed the second bottle that she was carrying to Keily. 'And this is for you, Judge Keily.' She smiled coquettishly at him. The musky perfume she wore reached to both men.

After feigning a brief interest, the dog had lain down tiredly in the street behind the girl, waiting for her to lead it back to its favourite spot.

'Most kind of you, my dear,' Keily replied. Unstopping the bottle he drank deeply, smacking his lips afterwards.

'There's a stranger riding up on us, Judge,' Oakes cautioned urgently.

'Let him come,' the judge said calmly, as he squinted at the approaching rider.

'Could be one of the boys from a ranch hereabouts,' Cora suggested. She hugged herself for a moment, rubbing her arms.

Tommy Oakes dismissed what she said with a shake of his head. 'There ain't no one about here rides a dun horse like that, Cora.'

'He's a right mean-looking cuss,' the judge observed as the rider came nearer. 'Best you go back down to the saloon and stay inside, girl.'

'Do you think he'll cause trouble?' the girl asked anxiously.

'Nothing we can't handle.' Oakes replied boastfully.

'I don't want you getting hurt, d'ya hear, Tommy?'

'I can take care of myself, Cora.'

'Right now, child,' Keily told the girl,

'you take care of yourself by skedaddling back down to the saloon.

The girl left them, her walk so graceful that it was a dance. When the dog realized she was going it stood up to lift one back leg to vigorously scratch at its yellow belly, then followed the girl. Occasionally she glanced back over her shoulder worriedly as she went.

The judge stepped out to hold up a hand, halting the rider. 'Hold it right there.'

Reining up, the rider stared steadily down at Keily. Then he cleared his right foot from the stirrup and rested the leg across the saddle in front of him. Taking the makings from his pocket, he rolled a cigarette deliberately slowly. Lighting it, he let it hang from the corner of his mouth as he looked questioningly from Keily to Oakes, then back to Keily again. Though his tanned face was expressionless, he had the kind of tough look that would make most men wary of him. Eyes narrowed against the smoke curling from his cigarette, he spoke so softly that it was close to a whisper.

'If you've good reason for stopping me, mister, you'd better state what it is, pronto.'

Unflinching, Judge Keily held the hard man's gaze. 'I'm Judge Keily, stranger, the principal representative of law and order in this here town. We have ourselves a bit of a scary situation here right now, and this makes me ask what business you got here in Tularosa?'

'My business is my business,' the rider answered tersely.

'Then if that's your attitude, stranger,' the judge said, 'I'm going to have to ask you to come down out of the saddle while I take a look through your saddle-bags.'

Ready to back the judge, Oakes shifted his shotgun into a waist-high firing position. Though not looking his way, the rider asked, 'You aiming to die young, kid?'

'I ain't no kid.' Annoyance crossed Tommy Oakes' tanned face like a shadow. 'I could blast you right out of that saddle.'

The rider gave a curt nod. 'I daresay you could, kid, but I'd still have time to kill you and Judge Riley.'

'Keily,' the judge corrected him. 'That would mean all three of us dead, which seems kind of pointless whichever ways I look at it. The boy's got a right to crow, stranger. It is him this town has to thank for putting a right dangerous bandit in jail. So, looking at it logically, I'd say that it would be best if'n you got down off that horse.'

Undecided, sitting absolutely still for a moment, the rider then dismounted.

2

Irritated by a growing thirst, Clancy stood sweating and motionless. Not having looked in the saddle-bags since taking the dead US marshal's horse, he had no idea what the result of the judge's search would be. Neither did he care. All he wanted was to be allowed into the town. Though he had enough money to last him for a week or two, he needed to reunite with the Paltroes as soon as possible. If the gang was about to hit the bank in Tularosa, then he wanted to be in on the raid. With that in mind he didn't want to do or say anything that would have him stick in the mind of the boastful Tommy Oakes or the officious Judge Keily. The hired gun needed to draw attention to himself and his calling, whereas the mark of a good bank robber was to go unnoticed. The judge was the type who wanted to know all about you in a couple of seconds. People in small towns had too much nose.

Cautiously glancing at Oakes to make sure that he had Clancy covered with his rifle, Judge Keily strode purposely toward the dun horse, each step causing his jowls to tremble. Pausing, he turned to issue Clancy with a warning. His face was red and glistened with sweat as he held up a pair of thick, fur-backed hands. 'I've broken necks with these before, stranger, and I'll do so again if you try to make any kind of a move. I have a duty to protect this town.'

'My neck isn't easy to break, Judge.' Clancy couldn't resist a snappy response. 'This could be your unlucky day.'

Not answering, Keily started to undo the straps of the first saddle-bag, but the deputy town marshal spoke for him. Oakes' trousers sagged and there were heavy sweat stains in the armpits of his light-coloured shirt. Giving his rifle a threatening little jerk, he told Clancy,

'Keep your mouth closed, stranger, or you could mighty soon get real unlucky yourself.'

'Speaking of luck,' the judge cried excitedly, as he pulled a shiny star out of the saddle-bag and studied it admiringly. Then he closed his eyes and gave a deep-rumbling giggle. 'I reckon as how this is a right lucky day for Tularosa and all the folk living in this great little town. Put down that rifle, Oakes. This here stranger is United States Marshal Ronan Lombard.'

Walking over to Clancy, the judge held out the badge in a trembling hand. Excitement added additional volume to his booming tones. 'Pin it on, Marshal, pin it on!'

'What's happening?' a bewildered Tommy Oakes asked.

Keily didn't reply. Impatient at Clancy making no attempt to take the badge from him, he fumbled with thick fingers to pin it on to Clancy's chest. 'Why didn't you say who you was first off, Marshal?'

Quiet a moment, groping for the best way to use this unexpected turn of events to the best advantage, Clancy decided to encourage the judge's mistake. In a town made desolate and fearful and suspicious by recent events, he'd get along better as a US marshal than he would as just another plains drifter.

'I always like to get the lay of the land before identifying myself, Judge,' he said.

'Very wise, very wise,' the judge agreed, clearly in awe of a man in the top lawman's position of US marshal. 'We're sure glad to welcome you to Tularosa. Folk here will sleep easier in their beds tonight knowing that you're in town. You'll want to be brought up to date, of course, so may I invite you to have dinner at my house this evening? You'll discover that my good lady wife is a wonderful cook.'

'That's mighty hospitable of you, Judge,' Clancy said. 'And I accept most gladly. Right now I'd best get myself fixed up at a hotel.'

'Then you won't do better than the Rest and Welcome, Marshal. Matt and Sadie Forston will make you real comfortable. Their place is on your right about half-way down the main street. Tell them that I sent you along.'

'I'll do that, Judge, and I thank you,' Clancy said, as he swung up into the saddle. But he couldn't risk riding on into Tularosa without knowing who it was being held for an appointment with the executioner. He couldn't ask Keily a direct question without arousing suspicion, as this would be information that a US marshal should already possess. So he resorted to subterfuge by asking, 'There's no doubt that the man you have in jail is who he said he is, Judge?'

'Not a shadow of a doubt, Marshal. It's Hank Paltroe right enough.'

Though he didn't show it, this news shook Clancy. He had ridden with the Paltroes for a long time, which meant that he would be expected to help free

Hank. If he didn't, then he would lose the means to earn a living, however unlawful. If he did, then his unasked for masquerading as a US marshal, and all he might gain from that, would be over.

As he moved his horse away at a walking pace, Clancy decided to play it by ear. He would remain as a US marshal for as long as the situation would permit. It was utterly quiet and oppressive, as he rode between Tularosa's big log buildings with steep roofs. The dusty street was as lonesome as Boot Hill. In the distance beyond the grass-choked valleys and high mesas were towering and bulky mountains, their peaks snow-crowned despite the overpowering heat in the town. Reining in, he dismounted outside of the impressive Rest and Welcome. The same rigid quiet held its spell here, too. The hotel was a two-storey building with a long veranda that had a shady balcony with green-painted wrought iron balustrades above.

Two old-timers dozing in chairs on

the veranda didn't stir as Clancy passed them to go into the lobby. The inside of the hotel was as impressive as the outside. A short man, obese and careless about how his clothes fitted him, was standing behind a mahogany desk. He was balding, with a ring of grey hair that circled his head like a wreath.

He looked up in surprise at Clancy's approach, and remarked, 'We don't see many strangers in Tularosa these days.'

'Are you Matt Forston?' Clancy asked.

Suspicion etched an expression of fear on the hotel man's round face. It revealed how on edge this town was, and Clancy spoke again to ease the situation, 'Judge Keily recommended your place.'

'Oh, I see.' The relieved hotelier managed a shaky smile. Catching sight of the badge on Clancy's chest, he seemed to have a problem dragging his eyes away from it. 'Yes, I'm Matt Forston. You want a room, Marshal. For how long?'

That was a question Clancy had asked himself without coming up with an answer. Shrugging, he replied, 'I can't say for sure. Maybe we could take it a day at a time?'

'Certainly. We aren't exactly over-whelmed with guests at the moment.' Opening a large book he thumbed through the leaves. 'I'd best get you to sign the register. Judge Keily is a stickler where that's concerned, par-ticularly in the current situation.'

Picking up a pen and dipping the nib in an inkwell as the hotel man turned the register round for him, Clancy began to sign his own name. Then, altering the *B* to an *R* and the *a* to an *o*, he penned the name *Ronan Lombard*, adding with a flourish, *US Marshal*.

Doing a quarter turn, Clancy looked through an arched doorway into the dining-room. There was the sound of the tinkling of cutlery and the hushed undertow of conversation from the few people sitting round one large table, eating. They looked like ranchers and local business people. There was not a drummer to be seen, which was more evidence of the town's ban on outsiders.

'Number Seven, our very best room, Marshal,' Forston fawned, as he pushed a key across his desk. 'First floor, second door on the right.'

Picking up the key, more conscious than ever of his raging thirst, Clancy enquired, 'Can I get me a drink?'

'Tea's being served in the dining-room right now, Marshal.'

Dismissing this with a shake of his head, Clancy said, 'I had a long, cool beer in mind, Forston.'

'We do have a nice little bar, but it doesn't open until eight o'clock.'

'I'll make my own arrangements,' Clancy said. He turned to look out into a street empty except for the dun horse that stood patiently, its head drooping. 'Can you have somebody take care of my horse?'

'Of course,' Forston replied, hitting the plunger of a brass bell with the palm of his hand to summon a young Negro.

Starting to climb the wide staircase, Clancy heard footsteps coming down. He looked up to see a woman with blonde hair that shimmered in soft waves to her shoulders. Though aware that he was staring rudely, Clancy couldn't help doing so. The woman had a kind of rare beauty that was as much internal as physical. It was an inner beauty carefully repressed in a way that made a woman compulsively attractive. A woman like her was special, and the dramatic lighting on the stairway somehow picked her out and projected her. For Clancy she was a reminder of something way back in his past. He couldn't place either when or what it was.

Stopping one stair above Clancy, she looked down at him with an uncertain smile.

'A new guest,' she exclaimed mildly. 'We don't see many strangers in Tularosa these days.'

'So I understand,' Clancy responded politely. 'I'm Ronan Lombard, ma'am.'

'US Marshal Lombard.' She gave him his title after a brief study of the badge he wore. 'I'm Sadie Forston. Welcome to the Rest and Welcome. I hope that your stay will be a pleasant one.'

'I don't doubt that it will, ma'am,' Clancy said, passing her and going on up the stairs.

The window of his room looked out over the street. By standing to one side and pressing the side of his face against the window frame, he could see the single-storey building that was the Tularosa bank. It looked to be closed for the day, or about to close, but it was difficult to tell in a town paralysed by fear.

A movement on his right caught Clancy's eye. It was Deputy Town Marshal Tommy Oakes swaggering down the middle of the street, his rifle tucked under his right arm. How could a raw youngster like that have overcome a man like Hank Paltroe?

That was a question to which Clancy had to find the answer pretty soon. There were a lot of other questions that also needed answering.

* ★ *

Madge Keily was uneasy as she watched Norman Spelling bolt the heavy door of the bank. Though slight, the grating noise of the sliding bolt jangled on her nerves. While accepting that the fussy little manager could take no chances the way things were in town, she felt trapped. Her working day was over but her father had ordered that she remain in the bank until Will Tarner, the local man with whom she could loosely be described as walking out, arrived to accompany her to her home. Judge Keily reasoned that as he was responsible for the jailing of a dangerous outlaw and for holding him until his execution, his daughter was vulnerable. If the gang should kidnap

Madge they could ransom her for Hank Paltroe. As a devoted father, Keily wouldn't hesitate in exchanging the desperado for his daughter. That would be hard for him to do, but the judge's love of law and order was surpassed only by love for his daughter.

Madge secretly considered that having Will as an escort was ludicrous. Though the young blacksmith was a giant with shoulders as wide as a barn door, and thick, heavily muscled arms, the Paltroe gang was likely to hit town with guns blazing. The physically powerful but slow-moving Will Tarner would never be a gunslinger. A hard fist was no match for a fast gun.

A loud knock on the door had Spelling hurry to the small window and peer cautiously out. Hurrying to the door, he reported to Madge as he went, 'It's young Will.'

The blacksmith had an adoring smile for Madge as he stepped into the bank. It spread slowly over his large, boyishly handsome face, reaching his blue eyes last. The sight of him always triggered off the old nagging doubt in Madge. Will's feelings for her were very evident, but she never ceased questioning herself on how she felt about him. Was Will Tarner the man she wanted, or was he no more than a compromise in the limited choice of a small town? A necessary compromise perhaps, as she didn't want to end up like the two Miss Stewarts who owned the haberdashery store. The only man in their lives was Preacher Willard at the church.

'I'm very worried, Will,' an agitated Norman Spelling was saying. 'A really tough-looking bad man has got past Judge Keily. I watched him ride in. He's across the street in the Forstons' hotel this very minute.'

Remembering the dark, menacing stranger, Madge could actually feel the tiny hairs rise on her forearms, and an icy-cold prickle ran down her spine. Her stomach muscles tightened involuntarily, causing a dull ache. Inside her mind, but sounding very far away, a voice said,

'I feel frightened, very frightened by this.' She silently answered back with a bogus confidence, 'Don't be silly. You worry too much. You have your father and Will to protect you. Nothing bad will happen.'

She supported what her employer had said. 'I saw him, too, Will. He has to be a member of that gang of outlaws. I don't mind admitting that I was alarmed by his appearance.'

'Don't you worry none about that man, Madge, or you, Mr Spelling,' Will Tarner assured them both. 'He's no renegade, but a United States marshal.'

'My word, that's a relief,' Spelling sighed, mopping at his shining brow with a brilliant white handkerchief.

Still not convinced, Madge gave a little shake of her head. 'He looked like a gunfighter to me.'

'You'll have a chance to change your mind when you meet him this evening,' Will smiled.

'This evening?' Madge frowned. 'I

thought that you were coming to dinner tonight, Will?'

'I am.' The blacksmith nodded his head of curly fair hair. 'Your daddy's invited the marshal, too.'

Why did the prospect of the hard-faced stranger coming to her home for dinner make her feel so ill at ease, Madge wondered, as she took Will's brawny arm when they were out on the street. They walked slowly around the courthouse square and sat together on a seat in the cooling shade of a giant cottonwood tree. She tried to keep her eyes away from the combination town marshal's office and jail. The violent death of Abel Turner, who had been a quiet, gentle lawman, still saddened her. Tommy Oakes ran the office now. It was worrying to realize that Oakes, young, foolhardy and inexperienced, was now the only law enforcement officer that Tularosa had. There were two jailers, Ed Skelton and 'Reedy' Williams, both elderly men who worked twelve-hour shifts so that the prisoner was guarded twenty-four hours every day.

This brought the prisoner to Madge's mind. She hadn't ever seen the man, and didn't know whether that was good or bad. Often the imagination produced images that were probably more harrowing than the true pictures. She had known and liked Abel Turner all of her life, but no matter what the condemned man had done, it was cruel that he had to sit in a cell day and night just waiting for the dreaded hour, being aware all the time just when that hour would come.

'You're quiet,' Will remarked.

'Am I?'

'Things will get back to normal once it's all over, Madge, and we'll all be a whole lot safer now there's a US marshal in town,' Will predicted, as they both idly watched Doris Stewart come out into the street to check a newly arranged window display. Dressed as always in sombre grey clothes, she put her head close to the glass, signalling instructions to her sister who was inside the window.

Seeing the spinster suddenly stiffen, her thin body going rigid, alarmed Madge. Then Doris Stewart hurried back to the shop door in an undignified run, losing her knitted grey shawl as she went. She paused, but only for a split second, then disappeared into the store, leaving the shawl lying crumpled on the sidewalk.

Wondering what had caused such a reaction in the calm, self-possessed woman, Madge noticed that someone had come out of the Rest and Welcome hotel, and she knew. It was the man whom Will had identified as a US marshal. Though the stranger was slender and neat-looking, there was an indefinable, distinctly menacing, air about him.

Madge was surprised to see him pause and look down at the abandoned shawl. Bending to pick it up, he laid it carefully on the sill of the store window before walking on. Heading directly for the Majestic Saloon, he vaulted over the hitching rail instead of walking round it. Landing lightly on his feet and springing lithely up on to the sidewalk, he went into the saloon.

As he went from her sight, Madge gave an involuntary, convulsive shudder, and clung tightly to Will Tarner's muscle-packed arm.

★　★　★

It was early, and when Clancy entered the saloon's long, broad room, it was empty except for a girl sitting on a redwood stool at the crude, hewn-log bar. Clancy glanced at his reflection on a huge, ornately framed mirror behind the bar. It pleased him that the badge didn't look out of place on his chest. A bartender came from somewhere out the back, and Clancy ordered a beer.

Studying Clancy steadily, the girl said, 'We don't see many strangers in Tularosa these days.'

'Is that a fact,' Clancy, bored by

repeatedly hearing the same comment, said with an obvious lack of interest.

Because of his habit, born of necessity, of checking out everything going on around him, Clancy recognized the girl who had been walking away, followed by a yellow hound, when he had ridden into town that afternoon.

Sliding down from the stool, she walked to stand by him at the bar. 'I'm Cora.'

Clancy accepted this information with a curt nod. The girl wasn't just pretty all over, there was something alive about everything she did. She seemed to be in touch with every part of her lithe young body. She struck a tough kind of pose with her thumbs in the thin leather belt at her waist.

'You don't have to buy me a drink, mister,' she complained, 'and being sociable don't cost nothing.'

Badly in need of the drink the bartender had poured him, Clancy tossed a coin on to the bar, picked up his drink and walked away from the girl without speaking. Needing solitude to prepare himself for dinner at Judge Keily's house, where things were bound to be tricky, he went to sit at a small table. His back against a whitewashed wall, he had a direct view of the door.

Not many minutes went by before the girl came toward him, a half-filled glass in her hand. Placing the glass on his table, she stood looking at him almost challengingly. The sun slanted through the window behind her, forming a crosshatch pattern on the hard-packed earthen floor. She gave a little self-conscious laugh before speaking.

'Like I said, you don't have to buy me a drink, mister, and being sociable don't cost nothing.'

Though he didn't regard any female below thirty-five as a real woman, Clancy had to admit to himself that the dancehall girl had something special about her. Whatever, he needed information and Cora's profession made her a likely source. He made a half apology. 'I have a heap of thinking to do.'

'That's for sure,' the girl said, her pretty face serious as she pulled up a chair and sat across the table from Clancy. 'Sooner or later that gang will hit town to rescue their *compadre*, and you'll have to face them all on your lonesome.'

'There's Judge Keily and that young deputy,' Clancy reminded her.

Cora looked at his face for a second, then she nodded. 'The judge ain't hardly a Billy the Kid, Marshal.' Silent for a moment, she then added, 'I suppose I shouldn't say it, what with him kinda being my boyfriend, but I don't reckon as how you should put too much stock in Tommy as a fighting man.'

'Oakes?' Clancy raised both eyebrows in surprise. 'To have got the better of Hank Paltroe, he has to be good, Cora, real good.'

'I don't know what you heard, Marshal, but you ain't heard it right.' Cora wrinkled her pert nose. 'I was on the street at the time and saw it happen.

It was a close thing between Abel Turner and Paltroe. Turner was faster on the draw, and his shot grazed Paltroe's head. I seen him stagger, but he was able to squeeze off a shot that did for Turner. When Tommy arrived, Paltroe was down on his knees, barely conscious.'

'So that's how the boy was able to lock up Hank Paltroe.' Clancy breathed out his words slowly, pleased that the girl had solved the riddle for him.

'Yep. Doc Harley spent a couple of hours patching up Paltroe's head. And I know for a fact that the outlaw didn't come round for a long time after that.'

Clancy found that his situation was easing. If, as sooner or later he would have to, he took the side of the Paltroes, then dealing with Tularosa's two men of law wouldn't be difficult. He remarked to Cora, 'It looks like you're right and I am on my lonesome.'

'Unless you want to count an old windbag and a young boaster,' she said with a delightfully tinkling laugh.

'Cora,' he began dramatically, 'I'd say it is time for me to buy you a drink.'

Running her tongue along the edge of white teeth, she spoke so quietly that it was scarcely audible, 'I reckon as how I'd find it easy to like you, Marshal Lombard.' Then she dropped her eyes quickly and turned her face away.

'I'm a real likeable *hombre*,' he told the girl jokingly to keep things light. Enjoying her company, he regretted having to leave her when it came time to ask directions to Judge Keily's house. Though he would rather have spent the remainder of the evening with Cora, it was important right then to keep on the right side of Keily.

In the setting of a tree-flanked lane and at a comfortable distance from Tularosa's Main Street, the judge's house was a grandiose southern colonial building. Uncertain that he could carry off his pose as a US marshal, Clancy reluctantly stepped up on to a wide veranda that had four white columns spaced equidistant along its length.

Taking a deep breath, he yanked on the cord of a brass bell. A male Negro servant wearing a dazzling-white jacket opened the door. Before Clancy had chance to explain who he was, an exuberant Judge Keily appeared behind him.

'Come on in, Marshal Lombard, come on in.' Keily boomed. He swung one arm in a sweeping gesture to indicate someone standing at his rear. 'We have another guest this evening. He is someone I would very much like you to meet.' He turned his head to speak over his shoulder. 'This is United States Marshal Ronan Lombard.'

Stepping inside, Clancy felt his skeleton turn from bone to ice as he found himself looking into the frowning face of a bewildered Gilbert the hangman.

3

'How soon will you be able to do the job for us, Gilbert?' Judge Keily asked over dinner.

'That will depend on many factors, Judge Keily,' Gilbert answered in his pragmatic way, 'not the least of which is whether you have a reliable carpenter in town?'

Listening intently to the conversation, Clancy regretted that worry was rendering an excellent meal tasteless. When the Judge had 'introduced' them, Gilbert had hesitated only briefly before shaking him by the hand and saying, 'I am very pleased to meet you, Marshal Lombard.' But Clancy could tell that the hangman was perturbed by his bogus identity. Gilbert was a man who liked everything to be exactly right, a fact that had Clancy wondering for how long he would support the pretence.

The judge replied confidently to Gilbert, 'You won't find a better craftsman than Nathan Powell. His place is down at the bottom of Main Street.'

'Mr Powell's skill as an artisan is, of course, important,' Gilbert acknowledged, 'but it is even more essential that he be prepared to take orders from me unquestioningly and work precisely to my specifications. I am a perfectionist, Judge Keily. I have invented a gibbet, a species of machinery that is unsurpassed in simplicity and which works absolutely faultlessly.'

'I'll see to it that Nathan does exactly what you require of him. If we take it as read that Nathan fills your requirements, Gilbert, how long would you estimate?'

'Really, Father,' Madge Keily objected, 'this is hardly a conversation for the dinner table.'

Clancy was seated across the table from the judge's daughter. In the pale-yellow light of the dining-room,

Madge's strong-featured face had a mature, unselfconscious kind of attractiveness, rather than being beautiful in a feminine sense. Dressed in a flaring black skirt and a white blouse, she had been fortunate in inheriting her father's intelligence and self-confidence, and her mother's refined manners and sweet personality.

Gwendoline Keily was a gracious hostess. She had smilingly explained to Clancy that when the family had special guests for dinner, she invariably gave cook the night off and personally attended to the catering. 'One of my little foibles,' she had giggled girlishly. She had accepted Clancy's complimentary remarks on the meal with a pleased little inclination of her head and a 'That is most kind of you, Marshal Lombard. May I in return say what a real pleasure it is to have a perfect gentleman like yourself as a guest.'

Diplomatically, Gilbert answered the judge's question without offending his daughter. 'If you will forgive me, Miss

Keily, I will reply to the question asked me, and then make no further reference this evening to either my occupation or the unfortunate matter that brings me to Tularosa. My answer, Judge Keily, is three days, four at the most.'

'The sooner the better. Then we can all return to normal,' commented Will Tarner, a young man whom Clancy had instantly dismissed as lacking in everything other than physical strength.

'Now you are extending the subject, Will,' Madge complained.

'That's an end to it, Madge my dear. No more talk of the execution,' the judge promised as, with the meal at an end, his wife served coffee. He turned to Clancy. 'We've taken certain precautionary measures here, which I will show you later. I learnt several tricks from Abel Turner, God rest his soul, and there are a few surprises in store for anyone thinking of attacking the jail. What are your plans, Marshal? I assume that you have to make the decision whether to wait in town for a possible visit from the Paltroe gang, or to go out in search of them?'

Clancy had the latter course in mind. It would be a dangerous situation if Josie Paltroe, having no idea that Clancy was in Tularosa, came riding in with his men to come face-to-face with him. The fact that Clancy was wearing a US marshal's badge would be an added complication. His hope was that he could locate Josie somewhere outside of town. That way they could plan the best way to free Hank.

'I'm going to ride out in the morning to take a look around, Judge,' Clancy said. 'Your mountain range caught my eye as I rode in. Is there a likely hiding place or two in the foothills?'

'More than one or two,' Will Tarner answered, before the judge had the chance to reply. 'There's so many places to hide out that it would take six months to root anyone out.'

'I imagine that you know where to look, Marshal Lombard,' Judge Keily said.

'I've learned a little about the gang's habits, Judge,' Clancy confirmed, without enlarging on the subject.

'Goodness knows how you do your job, Marshal,' Madge said, drawing a jealous look from her boyfriend, who then transferred the look, now loaded with venom, to Clancy. 'You are awfully courageous.'

'I never saw myself in that way, Miss Keily,' Clancy said truthfully. They looked hard at one another. It was no more than a second that look, but in their eyes, their expression, or whatever breath of a motion one makes if only to exist, live, breathe, they had communicated well with one another.

At the end of the evening, determined to leave at the same time as Gilbert, Clancy expressed his thanks to Judge Keily and his wife. Going out of the house he stepped down into the road with the hangman at his side when he heard his recently assumed name called softly.

'Marshal Lombard.'

Turning, he could see the vague figure of Madge Keily standing in the shadows to one side of the door on the veranda. Pausing, not wanting to lose Gilbert, he glanced questioningly at the hangman, who sensed his concern and said, 'Go ahead. I'll wait here for you.'

Clancy joined Madge on the veranda. She reached out as if to touch him, but snatched her hand back quickly before it could make contact. Speaking almost in a whisper, she thanked him for coming back, adding: 'I wanted to ask you a favour.'

'If it's something I can do, then I'll do it, Miss Keily.'

'You are very kind,' she said. A slight breeze stirred her hair, and he caught her perfume. 'I want to ask you to look after my father. He is a brave man, Marshal, too brave. When this Paltroe thing comes to a head, as it must, he will put himself in danger. He will be no match for those desperadoes, Marshal, and I fear for him.'

Unable to reply, Clancy wrestled with

his thoughts. A desperate conflict went on inside his head. Madge was a decent, honest girl who deserved honest reassurance from him. Yet he could offer her nothing because, when the lead started to fly, he would be with those who were against her father. She was anxiously awaiting his answer, and he was forced to make it a neutral one:

'I'll keep my eye on him, Miss Keily.'

Clancy could see that this wasn't enough for her. He was racking his brains for something else to say, some comfort to offer, when she suddenly looked startled. Clancy understood her alarm when he glimpsed the massive silhouette of Will Tarner in the lighted doorway. Leaning close, she whispered, 'Thank you,' and walked quickly to her boyfriend.

When Clancy rejoined Gilbert, the hangman fell into step beside him and they walked, not speaking, toward Main Street. When they were close to the courthouse, Gilbert slowed his steps.

'I have a bed in the jailhouse, Mr

Clancy,' he explained. 'I like to stay close to my work.'

'I wanted to thank you for going along with the US marshal thing, Gilbert,' Clancy said.

Gilbert's perpetual frown deepened. 'There was no alternative at the time, Mr Clancy, but I must say that I'm unhappy with it, very unhappy. Yet you must have your reasons for becoming an impostor, and they are your business. However, I will say that whatever game it is that you are playing, if it should compromise me in my work in any way, then you will no longer have my support.'

'I'll make sure that it doesn't interfere with your duties,' Clancy promised him. 'What I don't want it to do is prevent us from being friends, Gilbert.'

'We will have to see, Mr Clancy. We will have to see.'

Standing for a while, watching the hunched-shouldered figure walk away from him into the night, Clancy then turned and headed for the Rest and Welcome.

When he entered the lobby it was illuminated only by one oil lamp. Needing to adjust, he stood still for a moment. Being under a roof was always a shock at first to Clancy, who was used to carrying the sky about with him as he travelled. There was an almost eerie stillness in the hotel. Matthew Forston was bent over the mahogany desk, a stack of books on his right, a pen in his hand and a worried expression on his face as he wrote frantically in a ledger. So engrossed was the hotelier in his bookkeeping that he didn't notice Clancy pass by him and climb the stairs.

As Clancy approached his room the door next to it opened. Sadie Forston was framed in the doorway, her fair hair backlit by a lamp in her room. She was wearing a dress of black shiny material, and several long strings of pearls reached to below her bosom. Moving a little to one side in what was a clear

61

invitation into the room, she said, 'You look like a man who could use a night-cap, Marshal.'

Pausing, Clancy looked at her for a long moment: sorely tempted, greatly wary. His stay in Tularosa was a confusing entanglement of falsehoods, and he couldn't risk further complications. Moving away, he told her, 'I should look like a man who could use a night's sleep, ma'am.'

Angered by the rejection, her mouth tightened, the lips thinning into a straight line. With a final glare at Clancy, she closed the door. As he went to his own door his attention was attracted by a slight sound on the stairway. A shadow thrown up on the landing wall by the lamp below in the lobby seemed marginally to change shape. Clancy was convinced that Matthew Forston was lurking on the stairs.

That was the second Tularosa man furtively watching his woman that evening. It meant nothing to Clancy, who shrugged and went into his room, closing the door behind him.

* * *

Although Cora Caddo, out for her morning ride, appeared to be wandering aimlessly along the trail, she had a purpose in mind. From the window of her room above the saloon she had seen Marshal Lombard head out of town in the direction of the foothills. She now made her way through a clearing where aged willows stood among a newer growth. There was a strange regularity to the new trees that suggested man had planted them. Aware that wasn't so, Cora pondered on the quirks of nature as she rode along a trail that swept around the bottom of a small hill. There were more trees now and the sounds of the wood life followed her along. Reaching a fork in the trail, Cora reined in her borrowed horse and tried to fathom which way Lombard would have gone at this point.

She didn't really know why she was following the marshal. Maybe it was because he was a stranger; a real man compared to Tommy Oakes and Tularosa's other menfolk. Whatever, he had fascinated her during the short time they had spent together in the saloon last evening.

Moving silently in a circle that brought her to an area of grassy flatland, she pulled up her horse and sat in the shade of a yew tree. The ground had a slight rise ahead of her. It was very still here. Very quiet.

'Why are you following me?'

Startled by the disembodied voice, Cora looked around her. There was no one to be seen. It had to be the marshal who had challenged her, and she suddenly realized that she knew nothing about the man. Fear made her scalp prickle icily.

Then he stepped out from behind a cottonwood to stand immediately in front of her. Though he was unsmiling she was able to tell that he was no threat to her. Relaxing, she leaned over in the saddle to pull a shaft of wild wheat out of its coarse scabbard and chew on the sweet end.

'I ride every morning, Marshal,' she said lightly, dismounting to stand close to him. 'Alf, the boy who works at Mason's Livery, is a friend of mine. He always lets me have a horse.'

'So, you weren't following me?' he asked, an amused twinkle in his eye now.

All Cora could do was shrug. Lying to an astute and intelligent man like the marshal was pointless; neither did she want to jeopardize the opportunity to spend some time with him here. With bright sunlight slanting through the trees, it was a pleasant setting.

She looked at him coyly. 'As I said last night, I could get to like you, Marshal Lombard.'

'I'd welcome that, Cora,' he said, his eyes holding hers, thrilling her. Then he puzzled her by adding, 'But there's somebody who sure wouldn't like it if you and me got together.'

'I don't understand.'

'You're a town girl, Cora,' he smiled fondly at her, 'otherwise you would have noticed that there's been someone on your tail ever since you left Tularosa.'

'Are you sure? Why would anybody follow me?' Cora was shocked. The notion that she was being followed unnerved her more than it puzzled her.

Very aware of his comforting hand on her shoulder, she heard the marshal say, 'I'm sure. Whoever he is, he's up there somewhere on that lava-capped plateau behind you right now, watching us.'

'Could it be one of the outlaw gang trailing you, Marshal?'

He shook his head. 'I know when I'm being tailed, Cora.'

Cora's gaze went past him, drawn to something. The marshal was doubtless right that there was someone behind her, but there was also somebody in front of them. Ahead and above them on a higher track, the figure of a man moved across her line of sight. It was no more than a brown shadow that was quickly gone, but the marshal had noticed the change in her, and had turned in a smooth, fast movement. Cora knew that he had been quick enough to catch sight of the flitting shadow.

When he turned back to her his face had changed. He had a resolute expression that turned him from a charmingly handsome fellow that she liked into a hard man she didn't know. Cora was certain that they had caught sight of one of the Paltroe gang up ahead.

'Mount up and ride back to town, Cora,' he ordered her tersely.

'What is it?' she asked tremulously.

'It's nothing to concern you,' he replied. 'Am I right in thinking there's a lower trail going back into Tularosa?'

'There is, yes.'

'Then take it,' he advised. 'I'm pretty sure that whoever followed you out of town means you no harm, but he won't have time to come down and catch up with you if you get moving.'

Knowing that he intended to go on ahead to seek out the fleeting shadow worried her. But he was a different man; the sort of man with whom you didn't argue. So she swung up into the saddle and started back the way she had come. Whoever had been following her meant nothing now when compared to what the marshal might be about to face.

Aware of his eyes on her back, she looked over her shoulder when she topped a rise. She saw him walk to his horse and spring up on to its back in one agile movement.

* * *

As the couple far down below parted to ride off in opposite directions, Tommy Oakes rose up from where he had been lying flat so that he could see without being seen. The white-hot rage that had burned in him at seeing his girl with the marshal, was gradually cooling to the seething anger that had gripped him since being told that Cora and Lombard had been mighty friendly together in the Majestic Saloon. Having been Judge Keily's right-hand man and the law in town before Lombard had come riding in, Oakes had been pushed to one side. That was insult enough without having the marshal steal his girl, too.

Returning to where he had left his horse out of sight, he slid the rifle back into its scabbard and stood holding the reins, undecided. Cora having taken the lower trail meant that he couldn't ride after her to put her right about being his girl. Now he had a close to overpowering urge to follow the marshal and put an end to it.

All that restrained him was the awareness that Lombard, who was obviously a fighting veteran, would have an enormous advantage over him out here in the wilds. Oakes decided to postpone a showdown with the US marshal, but not for long. Judge Keily was relying on Lombard to keep the town safe until Hank Paltroe was hanged. But if the marshal continued making a play for Cora, Oakes would do something about it. He wasn't foolish enough to think he could out-draw the tough-as-leather new-comer, but there were other ways. Judge Keily would learn that Tommy Oakes was the only man he could truly depend on.

Up in the saddle, Oakes looked down from the plateau. Neither Cora nor the marshal were anywhere to be seen.

* * *

Ascending a slope toward a low mesa, Clancy dismounted, walking the dun horse to skirt an entanglement of fallen trees. Discovering that Cora was on his trail had brought home to him just how strange a place Tularosa was. The town had immediately plunged him into a complex situation by mistaking him for a US marshal. In this tricky situation he would prefer not to be pursued by the hero-worshipping Cora Caddo, and not to have the sultry Sadie Forston make unsubtle overtures. Madge Keily was the only woman in town who interested him. But Clancy would force himself to avoid her deliberately. Years ago, as a young renegade, he had learned that any romantic liaison in a town made capture at a later date more likely. A sheriff's posse gives up eventually, but the anger of a woman scorned is everlasting.

With Hank Paltroe condemned to death, and his brother lurking somewhere out here in the foothills, while the townsfolk were expecting Clancy to ensure their safety, he accepted that he was walking a dangerous tightrope. Engrossed in his thoughts, he was alerted by the crackle of leaves being stepped on. His right hand went automatically to the handle of his holstered .45.

Waiting for a minute or so, in which

time there were no further sounds, Clancy mounted up. Satisfied that some creature of the wild had made the noise, he eased the dun horse up a steep grade and swung into a narrow defile. The dun pressed on a little more swiftly as the grade levelled off into a canyon.

Too late, Clancy heard a hissing, swishing sound. An expertly thrown rope came fast through the air, the running loop at the end of the rope dropping over his shoulder. Effectively lassoed, Clancy had time to blame too much thinking and the expectation of only meeting Josie Paltroe and his gang, for his lack of alertness. Then the rope was pulled tight, pinioning his arms to his sides, and he was yanked out of the saddle.

Head slamming against a rock as he hurtled through the air, Clancy was unconscious when he hit the ground. When he came round he discovered that his arms were still bound tight to his body, and the other end of the rope had been used to lash his ankles.

Standing over him was a broad-shouldered man of around thirty who had a black moustache that was like an inverted horseshoe, the tips drooping below a prominent chin. He wore crossed gunbelts with a six-shooter in a tied-down holster at each hip. The grey eyes that looked down at Clancy were ice-cold.

'What are you doing poking around in these parts, lawman?' he asked, in a rasping voice.

Clancy didn't reply and, when the two-gun man bent closer to ask the question again, Clancy saw the cause of the unusual voice: a white scar across the man's throat, running almost from ear to ear. Standing upright, he lashed out with his right foot, the pointed toe of his boot catching Clancy hard in the ribs.

'I asked you a question, lawman.'

Seeing the foot drawing back ready to deliver a second kick, Clancy rolled to his right to protect his already painful ribs. Moving swiftly, the man stepped over Clancy, spun on his heel, and kicked him in the face. The impact of the boot against his jaw sent Clancy's brain spinning and rolled him back to his former position.

The man with the drooping moustache was back there to deliver another vicious kick to Clancy's ribs. Body racked by pain and the right side of his face agony, Clancy struggled hopelessly against the rope binding him. Needing to fight to keep a grip on consciousness, he heard boots scraping on rock as another man approached.

Somewhere, seemingly at the far end of the black vortex in which he was spinning, a voice asked, 'What's happening here, Kiowa?'

Fairly certain that he recognized the voice, Clancy found this helped him struggle back to full awareness. He heard the moustachioed man reply, 'I got myself a lawman, Josie.'

A relieved Clancy knew that he had been right about the voice, and he opened his eyes to see Josie Paltroe hunkering at his side, freeing him from the rope. Helping Clancy to his feet, Josie cursed at the black-haired man, then said, 'You danged fool, Kiowa. This here's Barton Clancy. He ain't no lawman.'

'He's wearing a US marshal's badge,' Kiowa said, defensively, as Clancy had difficulty keeping his feet.

Holding his ribs with one hand, pierced right through with pain each time he drew a breath, Clancy gently massaged his aching jaw with his other hand. Gradually the torture he was enduring receded, and he was able to lift his head high enough to look Paltroe in the eye. Kiowa was looking at him, and Clancy guessed he was sneering behind the heavy moustache.

'I'm right sorry that this happened, Barton,' Paltroe apologized.

'It was a genuine mistake,' Kiowa said, and then he laughed.

This was too much for the suffering Clancy. Needing to inflict the most damage possible, and remembering the moustachioed man's damaged vocal chords, Clancy came suddenly upright. His right arm snaking out fast, the heel of the hand caught Kiowa across the throat, right on the thick white scar. Releasing a gurgling scream of sheer agony, Kiowa went backwards like a man treading water, before crashing to the ground on his back.

A smiling Josie Paltroe put an arm round Clancy's shoulders and gave him a brief but affectionate hug. 'Welcome back, Barton, I've sure missed you.'

4

Sliding open the heavy drawer of the late Abel Turner's desk, Tommy Oakes used a non-committal grunt to answer an unheard question from Cora. Sitting on the wooden rail that separated the office from the jail area, the girl pouted sulkily because he was taking little notice of her. The yellow cur that followed Cora around constantly, lay curled on the floor close to her, softly snoring. Oakes had promised to go with her to Mandozanita Creek that afternoon. It was one of her favourite places, and with its sage-panoplied knolls, low ridges, small meadows and springy patches, it was ideal sage-hen hunting country. That was a sport that Oakes enjoyed, but it didn't hold any interest for him right then. He was after far bigger game. A different kind of excitement had been building in him

77

since a fragment of memory had popped into his head during the night. The face of US Marshal Lormbard had suddenly taken on a familiarity in his mind. This feeling had grown until he felt sure that he had seen Lombard's face on a Wanted dodger.

Keeping the bundle of notices inside the drawer so as to hide what he was doing from Cora, he sorted through them. Turner had been a hoarder, and many of the dodgers were outdated. Oakes went through about fifteen outlaws he knew to be dead, from natural causes or otherwise, before coming to those still living. After leafing through four of these he smothered a cry of delight, quickly disguising it as a cough. Staring up at him was a black and white image that was unmistakably that of the man whom Judge Keily and most folk in Tularosa had accepted as US Marshal Ronan Lombard. Under the photograph were the words:

BARTON CLANCY
WANTED FOR BANK ROBBERY
AND MURDER
SOCORRO, NEW MEXICO
$20,000 REWARD

Suppressing the urge to tell Cora of his discovery, he shut the drawer hastily and turned to her. She slid down daintily from the rail, causing the dog to stir just enough to open one enquiring eye. She asked, 'Are you ready to go now, Tommy?'

Shaking his head, Oakes replied, 'Sorry, Cora, but we'll have to put it off until tomorrow. I have to go find Judge Keily. Something mighty important has come up.'

'Something more important then me?' she challenged him angrily. 'You ought to be careful, Tommy Oakes. I could easily find someone else to take me down to Mandozanita Creek.'

Normally this would have had Oakes gripped by an almost insane jealousy, but now he grinned at the girl calmly.

'Like a certain US marshal?'

'You could be right,' she teased, enjoying the power she held over him. But she was bewildered and badly shaken, when Oakes laughed in her face.

Able to adopt a new, apparently uncaring attitude toward her, Oakes walked to the door, saying, 'Ed Skelton's out back. Cora. Have him lock the door behind you when you leave.'

⋆ ⋆ ⋆

What remained of the Paltroe gang was camped on high ground above the foaming, rippling waters of a brook. It was a small, natural fortress that could be reached only by a steep, rocky incline. Any approach would be spotted well in advance. Clancy rode beside Paltroe and Kiowa, with the reins of his horse in one hand and holding his damaged throat with the other hand, brought up the rear. As they neared the outlaw camp, Josie Paltroe cupped a hand over his mouth to imitate perfectly the long drawn cry of a sand crane. Seconds later he was answered by a similar call from the camp.

They rode in, and Clancy looked around as he dismounted. A taciturn, stoney-eyed Reb Hawker acknowledged Clancy's return with a curt nod, while the always-smiling Ike Short, deftly rolling a cigarette, wagged a welcoming finger at him. Clancy didn't dislike either of them, but each was as dangerous as the other in his eyes. The two of them were all that were left of the old band. An unperturbed Josie explained that the others had been unwilling to wait until Hank had been freed. The Tularosa bank was there for the taking, but not right away, so they had ridden off to rob elsewhere.

'We'll all get together again once Hank is back with us,' Josie predicted confidently. Indicating the newcomer with a nod of his head, Ike added, 'This *hombre* you had a run-in with is the

81

Kiowa Kid. He ain't spoken since you downed him, and I reckon there's a good chance he never will speak again. A Mex with a knife took away most of the working parts of his throat, and it's likely you finished off the rest.'

Looking to where the silent man skulked at the far side of the camp-fire, glaring menacingly, following every move he made, Clancy knew that the outlaw's code meant that a showdown between him and the Kiowa Kid had to come, most likely sooner rather than later. With a shrug of indifference, Clancy remarked, 'He shouldn't have jumped me, Josie.'

'I agree,' Paltroe nodded. 'Kiowa's new and pretty danged keen. I figure he's got a lot to learnt, but he's real good with a gun. He bears a grudge, so watch him, Barton. We don't want anything happening to you now you've set yourself up nicely in Tularosa.' With a bent forefinger he rapped the badge on Clancy's chest. 'That was a real good move.'

'I didn't ask for it, Josie. It just sort of happened. How come Hank got himself locked up?' Clancy knew Hank was not as intelligent as his brother, a fact that made him slightly less dangerous than the volatile Josie.

'Because my brother can be a danged fool at times.' Josie shook his head despairingly. 'He's always likely to go plumb loco when he's liquored up. He went into town to size up the bank, but got himself into a bust-up with some kid over a saloon gal. When the town marshal stepped in, Hank beat him to the draw. But it was a close thing and a bullet creased Hank's head and he was dragged unconscious into the jail.'

That was how Cora knew so much about the incident, Clancy reasoned, She was the girl over whom Hank had run into trouble, and Tommy Oakes, the deputy town marshal, was the kid with whom he'd argued. It was obviously a stupid confrontation that had had serious consequences.

'Hank sure loused things up,' Clancy commented.

'Nothing we can't fix,' Josie said, looking to the fire where Ike Short had roasted a rabbit and was making coffee. 'Come over and have yourself some grub, Clancy, and we'll work out what we're going to do.'

The smiling hospitality didn't fool Clancy. Josie Paltroe, a man whose mood could switch from amiability to viciousness in a flash, regarded everyone in his gang with suspicion. That included Clancy, who knew it was necessary to stay watchful. Anyone foolish enough to relax in Paltroe's company was in peril.

Hunkering at the fire, Clancy listened as Josie Paltroe outlined a plan to ride into Tularosa, break his brother out of jail, then knock over the bank before riding out of town.

'That won't work, Josie,' Clancy warned.

Long before Raimondo, Paltroe had feared he was losing what it took to be leader of the pack. That failed bank raid had increased his insecurity. Now he reacted aggressively to Clancy dismissing his plan before having heard it. 'You ain't been away from us long enough to forget who runs this outfit, Clancy. I give the orders, and if I say that's the way we're going to do it, then that's the way we're going to do it.'

Throwing the dregs of coffee from the mug into the fire, causing a hissing and raising a little cloud of steam, Clancy stood up, saying, 'Well, that's just fine, Josie, but you'll do it without me.'

Then he walked to his horse, intending to leave. Whatever Paltroe's plan was, it would be a repeat of the failed bank raid at Raimondo. It would be a disaster. Raimondo had put some of the most able members of the gang under the sod. Tularosa could be worse; likely to bring about the extinction of the whole Paltroe band.

'What happened at Raimondo could have happened to anyone,' Josie said, guessing what was on Clancy's mind as he walked slowly away from him. 'You need me.'

That was true. One man on his own couldn't hit a bank or rob a train, and any stagecoach worth holding up would be too well protected for a lone outlaw to handle. But Paltroe wasn't taking Tularosa seriously enough. Judge Keily was a wily old boy. Probably the braggart Tommy Oakes didn't know it, but the judge was probably using him as nothing more than a false front. Having checked out the buildings clustered round the town's jail, Clancy was convinced that Keily had men with rifles positioned in the upper windows. They were probably ordinary townsmen and cowboys rather than gunfighters, but there would be enough of them to cut down any number of men riding up to the jailhouse.

Clancy accepted that if he split from Josie Paltroe he wouldn't have the sort of money he was accustomed to, but at least he would be alive.

'Take one more step, Clancy,' Paltroe

called threateningly, 'and I'll drop you.'

Sensing that Josie had stood up Clancy stopped but didn't turn. Every inch of him keyed up to a piercing alertness, he asked, 'In the back, Josie?'

'No chance of that. Barton. You're fast. By the time I clear leather you'll have turned and drawn that Colt of yourn.'

Clearly seeing the situation he had created, he swiftly cooled the white-hot anger in Paltroe. Clancy waited, aware that the gang tacitly accepted that he was the brightest in the game of wits that was the robbery business. He could understand Josie's frustration. Always the leader, it was difficult for him to put himself in another man's hands in a matter as delicate as this.

Paltroe moderated his tone in a bid to ease the tension. 'I spoke out of turn, Barton. We've become kind of partners over the years. Come back and squat down. We'll talk this thing through together.'

Aware that it would be foolish not to

accept Paltroe's invitation, Clancy was about to turn when an always-reliable sixth sense reacted to a sound behind him. Even before Josie had hissed warningly, 'Clancy,' an instinctive reaction had Clancy crouch and turn, gun clearing the holster as he did so. The Kiowa Kid had seized his chance of revenge. He was fast, but his bullet went close past Clancy's head as a slug from his .45 shattered Kiowa's heart. Blood pumped from the hole in the outlaw's chest as he pitched forward face down in the fire, knocking over the coffeepot.

'I told you he was a *hombre* to bear a grudge,' Josie said calmly, as Clancy holstered his gun. 'Maybe you did us a favour, Barton. I don't reckon as Kiowa was ever going to fit in.'

There was a smell of burning flesh and hair. Cursing under his breath, Reb Hawker hooked the toe of his boot under the dead man to roll him out of the fire. Retrieving the coffeepot, cursing loudly again as it burnt his fingers, he threw it at Ike Short, with the guttural command, 'Make some more.'

Catching the pot, a smiling Ike juggled it to avoid the heat, as Josie signalled for Clancy to take the place he had previously occupied. 'Now there are just four of us, Barton.'

Though he had, out of necessity, killed many times himself, Clancy had always been appalled by the Paltroe brothers' callous attitude to sudden death. Looking to where the Kiowa Kid, his face horribly disfigured by the fire, lay on his back staring up at the sky through sightless eyes, he said, 'Every man, regardless, deserves the dignity of a decent burial, Josie.'

'Like all of us who live our kind of life, Barton, the Kiowa Kid had no illusions about how his would end,' Paltroe stated unfeelingly. He went on to complain, 'But you always did have too much good manners and such-like.' He beckoned Ike Short over, telling him, 'Plant the Kid over yonder, Ike.' Turning his head to face Clancy again, he asked, 'Four of us; are we enough to take care of things in Tularosa?'

'If we do it right,' Clancy nodded.

The unstable Josie Paltroe was calm and peaceable again now. Accustomed to the gang leader's rapid changes of mood, Clancy waited for him to speak.

'It's your call, Barton.' Josie said. 'You know the town now.'

Taking the mug of coffee that Ike Short passed to him, Clancy said, 'Tularosa looks easy to take, but I reckon otherwise.'

'You always was a cautious kind of cuss,' Josie remarked with a grin.

Shrugging, Clancy said, 'Like I said a while ago, Josie, you either do it my way or you do it without me.'

'I hear you,' Josie acknowledged.

Satisfied, Clancy spoke tersely. 'You try to rush the jail-house and you'll all die before you get within ten yards of the place.'

'Are you saying that we can't get Hank out?'

'You're poor shakes as a listener,

Josie,' Clancy complained. 'There's a hangman in town, and he'll be ready to take care of Hank in a day or two. On the morning the hanging's due, I'll see that there's a horse waiting for Hank at the back of the jailhouse. At the time they bring Hank out into the yard to the scaffold, you and your boys kick up a shindig, do a lot of shooting, at the bottom end of town. That will draw all attention in that direction. I'll tell them that I'm going to secure Hank back in the jail.'

'Only you don't, you let him out the back,' Josie chortled.

'You've got it.'

'That's great, Barton. Then we knock over the bank before leaving town.'

Clancy shook his head. 'No. There will be too many guns still covering the street. We go back the next day when we won't be expected. That way I figure we can hoist the bank without firing a shot. We'll be coming in from the south, and there's no window on that side of the bank.'

'I'm still for hitting the bank on the same day,' Josie argued. 'We'll have Hank, so there'll be five of us.'

'And all five of us will be cut down in the street,' Clancy told him grimly. 'When we get Hank out of town, he stays out, Josie. If we fetch him back in the next day, he'd be recognized straight away.'

'Dang it, Barton,' Josie protested. 'We'll need Hank's gun if something should go wrong.'

Clancy was adamant. 'Everything *will* go wrong if they see Hank. Listen, Josie. I'm going back into town now. In the forenoon tomorrow, I'll take a look inside the bank. I want to look things over awful careful. Later in the day, I'll ride back out here and we'll put the last details together. By that time I should know what morning they intend to hang Hank.'

Josie Paltroe walked with Clancy to his horse. As Clancy swung up into the saddle, the gang leader regarded him coldly through slitted eyes and said, 'We need funds, so this bank is important, Clancy, but saving my brother from the gallows is most important of all to me. If you get it wrong, and Hank gets strung up, then I'll kill you.'

'You mean that you'll try to kill me, Paltroe,' Clancy said. As he reached for the reins, Clancy was gripped by a cold anger. He had a need to get down from the horse and settle things with Josie Paltroe right then. They were so equally matched at the fast-draw that it could well be his last act on earth, but it was a matter of principle. But then a flash of sense cut through the red curtain of his rage.

He stared steadily into Paltroe's eyes for a long time. The seconds dragged by and only the chomping of Clancy's horse broke the stillness. Then Clancy pulled on the reins to turn and ride away, unhurried, letting his horse make its own gait.

★   ★   ★

After unsuccessfully searching the town, Tommy Oakes had found Judge Keily meditatively smoking a cigar on the porch of his house. The judge refused to believe Oakes's assertion that the man he knew as US Marshal Ronan Lombard was really a renegade named Barton Clancy. But now, at Oakes's insistence, they went into the jailhouse together, where Oakes hurried over to the desk and pulled open the drawer.

He reached in to take the reward poster that was on top of the pile, passing it to the judge. A wide grin spread across Oakes's face as Keily took the dodger and studied it. Oakes's pleased grin died a slow and miserable death as, with a scornful grunt, the judge handed the notice back to the deputy town marshal.

'You claimed that the marshal's name is really Clancy,' Keily said.

'That's right, Judge.'

'The name, on this handbill is McRee, and he doesn't look anything like Marshal Lombard.'

Almost snatching the dodger from the judge, Oakes stared at it closely before muttering a curse. Pulling the complete stack of reward notices from the drawer, he spread them on the desktop and sorted through then feverishly. Not finding what he wanted, Oakes said accusingly, 'Cora.'

'Cora Caddo?' the judge asked. 'What has that girl to do with it?'

'She was here when I found the dodger,' an angry Oakes replied. 'She must have taken it.'

'Why on earth would she do that, Oakes?'

'I think I know why. What are you going to do about it, Judge?'

'About the Caddo girl? What is there to do? You have no proof that it was she who took the handbill.'

Dismissing this with a vehement shake of his head, Oakes tossed the dodgers back into the drawer and slammed it shut. 'I didn't mean Cora. I was asking what you are going to do about the man pretending to be a US marshal?'

'I do not doubt for one moment that US Marshal Ronan Lombard is exactly who he claims to be,' Judge Keily said before turning to stride out of the door.

*　*　*

The three of them stood watching Clancy ride away from them far down below. He disappeared behind the shoulder of a knoll then reappeared, indistinct in the distance. All three of them gave a sudden, startled jump as a huge buzzard rose up from a bunch of greasewood and soared above them ponderously.

'Have you planted the Kiowa Kid, Ike?' Josie Paltroe queried.

'He ain't exactly six feet under,' Ike Short answered, wearing his habitual smile. 'But he's far enough down not to make a meal for that pesky buzzard.'

Picking up a stone, Reb Hawker threw it up at the bird without effect. He told Paltroe, 'Kiowa don't worry me at all, Josie, Clancy sure does. He was ten times faster than a striking rattler when he gunned down the Kiowa Kid. Are you going to go along with him?'

'Only so far as it suits me, Reb,' Paltroe replied, with a crafty expression on his lean, bony face. 'There's no future for Clancy with us. I reckon that he sure let us down in Raimondo, and I ain't ever going to give him a chance to do it again. I'll get from him the date on which they plan to hang Hank, and let Clancy believe that we're going to do as he says. But we'll hit the jail soon as they bring Hank outside that morning, then we'll take the bank. Clancy's always been one to see dangers where there ain't none. Tularosa ain't got nobody defending it other than a shaky old judge and a kid deputy town marshal who's way too big for his boots.'

'Maybe Clancy will help them out,' Ike Short smiled.

Looking out to where the diminutive figures of a man and a horse came out of an arroyo on to sage-dotted flats,

Josie Paltroe said quietly and absently, 'I'll be taking care of Clancy before he gets a chance to help anyone.'

* * *

Twilight was turning Tularosa into an undulating purple sea as Clancy rode back into town past the dead poplars that stood like sentinels along each side of the trail. He had hoped that his meeting with Josie Paltroe would resolve his problems. But it had only served to make him uneasy. Though Paltroe had agreed to rescue Hank the way he had advised, and to postpone the bank raid for at least a day, Clancy had misgivings. He was aware that Josie had come to see him as a threat to his leadership, as his likely successor. That being so, he couldn't afford to let Clancy's plan be successful here in Tularosa.

Entering the town, Clancy saw a light burning in the jailhouse and considered calling in to see Hank Paltroe. In two or three days, Hank would be shaking hands with Gilbert the hangman and led to the scaffold. Clancy needed to explain to him what was to happen once he was taken out into the yard of the jail.

But it was late in the day now. Deciding to put off his visit to Hank until the next morning, Clancy rode slowly on. Though attracted by the bright lights and the sound of music coming from the Majestic Saloon, Clancy resisted the temptation, and passed by to continue to the livery. Unsaddling the dun horse, he took care of the animal and settled it for the night before walking to the hotel.

There was no one behind the hotel desk, but Clancy could see a smiling Matthew Forston dispensing drinks at a small bar at the far end of the dining-room. The hotel proprietor didn't seem to notice Clancy passing by the open door.

Reaching the landing, Clancy silently cursed as the door on his left opened and Sadie Forston stood smiling seductively at him in the lamplight. In a husky voice she said, 'You've been out of town all day, Marshal: I've missed you.'

This worried Clancy. Having a woman watching you meant trouble. When it was a married woman, trouble with a capital T could be expected. Judge Keily had recommended the Rest and Welcome, but Clancy made an instant decision to move elsewhere in the morning. Sadie Forston was a dangerous woman. He went to pass her by, but she stayed him by placing a hand on his arm.

'I have a feeling that you won't refuse my offer of a drink tonight,' she said enticingly.

Very aware that to rebuff her could cause him a problem greater than accepting her invitation, Clancy accepted that he had to handle the situation carefully. He said, 'It is most kind of you, Mrs Forston . . . '

'Call me Sadie.'

'Please don't consider me rude, Mrs Forston, but I'm very tired,' Clancy excused himself. 'Perhaps some other time. Good night.'

Walking on, he was stopped dead in his tracks when she said quietly, but in a menacing tone, 'I think we should have that drink together right now — Mr Clancy.' When he turned to face her, she smiled. 'I overheard that boy, Tommy Oakes, telling Matthew that he had discovered who you really are, Barton Clancy.'

Sure of herself now, she stood with her back against the doorjamb, one hand daintily gesturing him into a perfumed and expensively furnished room. Closing the door, she turned the key and held out her hands. 'Let me take your coat.'

Meekly obeying her, Clancy sat in the chair she pointed to. Uncomfortable in the intimately feminine surroundings, he sat stiffly as she began pouring drinks from a crystal decanter. She stopped what she was doing, briefly as alarmed as Clancy was on seeing the door handle move. Someone pushed lightly against the door, discovered it was locked, and moved away. Clancy heard the sound of light footsteps going down the stairs.

Her moment of fright over, Sadie Forston came toward him, a sultry took on her lovely face, and a full glass of whiskey in each hand.

5

Most folk make the mistake of thinking that a brutal man must be of thuggish appearance, Clancy mused as Hank Paltroe saw him coming and came forward to hold the bars of his cage with both hands. The set of his broad shoulders was familiar to Clancy, although the narrow line of Hank's waist appeared alien without a gunbelt and an ivory-handled gun. As always, his dark eyes glittered like diamonds, and his roundish, sun-tanned face was as handsome as ever. Hank's wide mouth was continuously set in a way that suggested he was thinking of something pleasant. He had the looks of a charming gentleman, but the nature of a ruthless killer.

Hank's surprise at seeing Clancy changed to absolute astonishment as he caught sight of the US marshal's badge.

Pointing to the badge, he remarked humorously, 'I can't figure whether you've come to help me or hang me, Clancy.'

'I could do either, so don't tempt me, Paltroe,' Clancy said bluntly.

On the way to the jail that morning Clancy had seriously considered saddling up and riding away from Tularosa, the Paltroe gang, and all the problems that beset him. Sadie Forston had added considerably to those problems. Her husband had skulked scowling in the background when Clancy had eaten breakfast that morning. It had to be Matthew Forston who had tried the door that Sadie had locked after inviting Clancy into her room.

Even so, Clancy had decided to stay at the hotel. If he moved out he would still be in Tularosa so nothing would be solved. Most worrying had been the news from Sadie that Deputy Tommy Oakes had discovered his identity. All that Clancy could do was carry on in the way a US marshal would be expected to, including calling on the condemned man. Then it was a matter of waiting to see what happened. If, or probably when, he was challenged, he would need to think fast. He considered it best not to mention any of that to Hank Paltroe.

'You never was an easy *hombre* to get along with, Clancy,' Paltroe remarked, in his deceptively mild way. 'Seeing as how you're strutting around as a US marshal, all you need to do is to say that you are taking me to Santa Fe to be hanged, and we can ride out of here.'

'It isn't like that, Hank. Tularosa has brought in a hangman to do the job here.'

Paltroe couldn't see any problem. 'That don't stop you from saying that you're taking me into custody. As long as you're toting that badge I can safely walk out of here with you.'

'We'd both be cut down in seconds if we tried that,' Clancy said. 'I checked out the street as I walked here, Hank. Judge Keily isn't taking any chances where you are concerned. There's a rifle in just about every top window. I've met up with Josie and we've agreed how to get you out of here.'

'When?'

'The morning when they are about to hang you.'

'No. That's too risky. It has to be before that,' Paltroe protested. 'What if something holds you up, even by a minute or two? My head will be in the noose before you get here.'

'That won't happen, Hank. I'll be here with you all along.'

'I still don't like it,' Paltroe said.

'You'll have to learn to like it, Hank,' Clancy said, coldly, as he turned to walk away.

★　★　★

'Could you advise me here please, Mr Spelling?' Madge Keily asked desperately.

Having spread various papers and letters out on the counter between them, Gilbert had confused her with his wordy requests. Her father, who headed the committee that ran the town of Tularosa, had deposited Gilbert's fee with the bank. But payment to Gilbert depended on a number of conditions; the most important of which was that the money would not be transferred to the hangman until after the successful dispatch into the hereafter of one Henry John Paltroe.

'I would stress, Miss Keily,' Gilbert said earnestly, 'that if I should be afflicted by any of the seven deadly sins, avarice is not one of them. It is a matter of record that when thirty Indians were to have been hanged in the State of Nebraska, I communicated with Washington and offered to pay my own expenses, solely for the purpose of demonstrating how with the use of a gallows I had patented, thirty persons could be worked off at once. However, to my chagrin, President Johnson granted pardons to nearly every one of the Indians, so my invention could not be put to the test.'

'Is there some difficulty, Miss Keily?' Norman Spelling hurried to Madge's side to enquire.

Gilbert answered for Madge. 'There is no problem whatsoever, sir. I related that story to Miss Keily simply to illustrate a point.'

'What story is that?' Spelling enquired.

'I will tell it to you later, Mr Spelling,' Madge said, quickly, to forestall any chance of Gilbert repeating his monologue.

'My work means much more to me than the payment I receive for carrying it out,' Gilbert explained. 'Nevertheless, like all mortals I do have to eat and avail myself of certain creature comforts, and a principal character fault of mine is stubbornness. If Tularosa is unable to meet my financial requirements, then I shall not hesitate to leave the good folk of Tularosa to find another means of dispatching the murderer it holds captive. I will do so with regret, for though the nature of my calling more than suggests a certain callousness, depravity even, I in no way enjoy the taking of life. My purpose is to spare the agonized death I have witnessed uninformed executioners inflict on the condemned.'

As Gilbert finished speaking, the door of the bank opened and US Marshal Ronan Lombard entered. Very aware of his presence, Madge was embarrassed to notice that she was holding herself stiffly and her movements were jerky.

'I'll attend to Mr Gilbert,' Spelling said with a small sigh. 'You deal with the marshal, if you would be so kind, Miss Keily.'

Terribly conscious of the fact that she was blushing, Madge moved down the counter to face the marshal. Despite her having tried constantly to banish him from her thoughts, the handsome Lombard had been in her mind since he had come to the house for dinner. Will Tarner had noticed that something was different about her, and the intuition that often accompanies jealousy made him more than suspect that she was attracted to the US marshal.

Her father's liking for Ronan Lombard had influenced her greatly. Never a man to give praise lightly, the judge had told Madge and her mother, 'Too often you find a law officer can't resist the temptation to misuse the power bestowed upon him. But Marshal Lombard is different. He is a conscientious citizen interested only in following faithfully his oath to enforce justice.'

Removing his Stetson, an act that made him look younger and less tough, the marshal greeted her respectfully. 'Good morning, Miss Keily.'

Madge was conscious of the lawman's surprise at seeing her behind the counter. It had the effect of robbing him of much of the poised, self-possessed manner that had impressed her when he had taken dinner at her house. This had to be a reaction to her, and she was pleased.

'Good morning, Marshal. What can

the bank do for you today?' Madge self-consciously returned the greeting.

'I'm here on US marshal's business. I didn't know that you were with the bank, Miss Keily,' Clancy began, seemingly having recovered his self-confidence.

'It didn't come up in conversation over dinner,' she said, smiling. 'I started here at the bank straight from school.'

'Then I know where to come when I want expert advice.'

'I wouldn't claim to be an expert, Marshal.' Madge's cheeks burned and she realized miserably that her face must be bright red. 'What is it that you wish to say?'

'I have no wish to alarm you, Miss Keily, but as the Paltroe gang specializes in bank robbery, I wanted to cover all possible eventualities should they hit town. Is it just you and that gentleman here at all times?'

'Mr Spelling, yes, just the two of us. Do you believe that the bank could be threatened, Marshal?'

'Probably not, Miss Keily, but as a precaution I will ask the judge if he can muster some armed men to be positioned nearby.'

Pleased by this, Madge said, 'My father has had much support. Geoff Arthur has loaned ten Lazy L men to protect the town, and the smaller ranchers have provided eight men between them. I am fairly certain that I heard my father say that Mr Arthur will send in more men if required.'

'That's good,' Clancy nodded. He looked across to where Gilbert was animatedly emphasizing a point to Spelling. 'I'll speak to the judge later today, Miss Keily. I don't want to interrupt bank business, but I would be grateful if you could tell your colleague — '

'Employer,' a modest Madge corrected him.

'If you would tell him what I have in mind, please,' Clancy continued. 'I'll leave you to your work now, and hope to see you again soon, Miss Keily.'

'I think that my father intends inviting you to dinner again this evening, Marshal,' Madge stammered. She averted her eyes, staring absently out of the window down the dusty main street of Tularosa toward the mountains.

'That is very kind. But I will be most disappointed should you not be there, Miss Keily.'

'I'll be there,' she promised, and hearing the excitement in her voice made her aware that she had to be blushing even more deeply than before.

★   ★   ★

Stepping out into the street, Clancy was in a quandary. There was no problem with the bank, which was wide open and practically volunteering to be raided. But Madge Keily being employed there changed everything for him. Though he had always been careful never to kill or injure an innocent citizen when knocking over a bank, the same couldn't be said for the Paltroes or any other member of the gang. He felt so guilty about lying to Madge about arranging to have armed men in position to protect the bank, that it told him that he wouldn't be able to put her at risk in a raid.

But what alternative did he have? Like the others, he was in need of money, and Josie Paltroe would not agree to the raid on the bank being cancelled. Neither was there any way without raising suspicion that he could arrange for Madge not to be in the bank at the time.

'Marshal Lombard.'

Dashing out of the bank behind him, Gilbert had called urgently. Clancy turned, waiting for the hunch-shouldered hangman to come up to him. A grave expression on his face, Gilbert's strangely tilted eyes looked directly into his. By now accustomed to Gilbert's habit of carefully considering what he was about to say before speaking, Clancy waited patiently.

Lowering his voice, the hangman

asked, 'Are you at this moment returning to the Rest and Welcome, Mr Clancy?'

'I am.'

'They are waiting there for you.'

'Who is?' Clancy enquired tersely.

His habitual frown deepening as he tried to recall a name, Gilbert answered, 'That boy who helps Judge Keily. He's some kind of town marshal — '

'Tommy Oakes.'

'That's him,' Gilbert confirmed. 'You must get out of town, Mr Clancy. He knows who you really are, and he's waiting with a rifle at the hotel.'

This was a turn of events likely to change everything. Deprived of his cover as a US marshal, Clancy would neither be able to free Hank Paltroe as planned, nor protect Madge Keily, the girl of whom he had become very fond. Josie Paltroe would come galloping into town with guns blazing, and Clancy would have no choice but to ride at his side.

He asked sharply, 'Is the judge with him, Gilbert?'

'No. Judge Keily is not present, Mr Clancy. But there is a big young man there. I seem to think that he is the town's blacksmith. To the best of my observation, this second man does not seem to carry a gun of any kind.'

'Thanks, Gilbert,' Clancy said, slapping the hangman on the shoulder. The big and slow Will Tarner would cause him no problem. But Oakes would be as dangerous as anyone else behind a rifle would. 'I'd better not keep them waiting.'

'You must take care, Mr Clancy. Great care.' Gilbert took a heavy watch from his jacket. Flicking it open, he studied it for a moment before clicking it shut and replacing it in his pocket. 'I am meeting Mr Nathan Powell to begin constructing the scaffold. My device is far more complicated than the vulgar system that the public has become familiar with. That being so, its construction requires a considerable amount of my time and demands great concentration. Having said that, it would be remiss of me not to make time to go with you to the hotel.'

'I appreciate the offer.' It required exceptional courage for a man with no fighting ability to volunteer as Gilbert had, and Clancy was full of admiration for the man. Squinting against the bright sun, he asked, 'Why are you prepared to help me, Gilbert?'

A shrug lifted Gilbert's misshapen shoulders a little higher. 'I really can't answer that question, Mr Clancy. On the face of it we have little if anything in common. Yet in some odd way I feel that we are kindred spirits, fellow travellers on the hazardous trail through life, so to speak.'

'I'd like to think that we are, Gilbert,' Clancy said sincerely. 'We will meet again later today.'

Looking intently and silently at Clancy for a long moment, Gilbert then spoke hoarsely, 'I pray that the good Lord will spare you to make that possible, my friend.'

* * *

Having suffered the wrath of her husband since first thing that morning, Sadie Forston had sought sanctuary in the hotel kitchen. She just couldn't bear his constant accusations about the US marshal any longer. The accusations were both unwarranted and unfounded. That being so, she was honest enough with herself to acknowledge that this was due to the man she now knew to be Barton Clancy. Having listened to her warning about Tommy Oakes he had, coldly but politely, unlocked the door and gone out of her room.

The rift between her and Matthew that morning was an extension of their long and acrimonious relationship. They had met in Lobo Flats, where Sadie had been living what wasn't much of a life in what wasn't much of a town. They met when Matthew had called at the Paris Saloon as a highly successful drummer for a whiskey firm. Instantly smitten by her, Matthew had stunned her with a proposal of marriage. She had made an attempt at explaining to him that she hadn't always been a saloon girl, but an adoring Matthew had stroked her hair, lovingly touched her cheek, and told her that he was not troubled one bit by her occupation.

That had been true, but only until a week later when they had married. No church had been built in Lobo Flats, so they were wed in the preacher's house, which was no more than a shack. Word of the wedding had got around, and when the Reverend Wall, a tall, sombre figure in a long black coat had finished the ceremony, friends wanting to wish her well had mobbed Sadie. Her group of well-wishers had been largely comprised of cowboys from the surrounding ranches. At that moment, Matthew had been consumed by a crazy jealousy that had blighted their lives ever since.

Matthew had used his savings to retire from his salesman job and buy the Rest and Welcome Hotel, but their move to Tularosa had not solved their marriage difficulties. He constantly reminded Sadie of her lowly status before he had married her. Each time he refused to let her tell him of her former life as an actress in New York, and the circumstances over which she had no control that had caused her downfall.

Now keeping busy by helping Juanita, the elderly cook, an anxious Sadie kept the door slightly ajar so that she could see what was happening in the hotel lobby. Matthew was still in a foul mood, and she could see him stamping angrily about behind the desk.

The sight of Tommy Oakes coming into the hotel alerted her. The young deputy town marshal had a rifle under his arm; the powerfully built but unarmed Will Tarner was at his side, a purposeful look on his face. His yellow hair, worn long, curled out from under the back of his black Stetson as he strode up to the desk and said something to her husband.

A conversation followed that Sadie

couldn't hear. But the blood in her veins turned ice-cold as Matthew reached under the desk to bring up a Navy Colt. With the self-satisfied smirk on his face that she had come to hate, he held the weapon up, demonstrating to Oakes and Tarner that it was loaded. Then Matthew carefully replaced the gun in its former concealed position under the desk. She knew that the three of them were waiting for Clancy to return. With Oakes and his rifle facing him, and Matthew Forston and his gun behind him, Clancy wouldn't stand a chance.

Watching and waiting, Sadie seized her opportunity when Oakes and Tarner were standing together in the hotel doorway looking out, and Matthew had gone hurrying up the stairs on some errand. Swiftly and noiselessly, Sadie hurried to the desk. Keeping a watchful eye on the two men in the doorway, she bent down and her groping fingers touched the cold butt of the Colt. She was about to pick up the weapon, when her husband's shout stopped her. Filled with fear, she froze, still bending over with her hand under the desk.

'Sadie! What are you looking for?'

She hadn't heard him coming back down. He was standing on the third stair up, suspicion on his face as he waited for her reply.

'I was . . . I was just . . . I was just looking . . . ' she stuttered, searching her mind for something that sounded like a valid excuse. 'I just wanted to check the guest list to see how many we have for lunch.'

Matthew didn't believe her. That was obvious from the look on his face. Descending the last three stairs he started toward her. 'I have already told Juanita how many lunches she needs to prepare.'

'I didn't know that. I'm . . . I'm sorry. I'll just ..'

Tommy Oakes became Sadie's unlikely saviour. He and Tarner came hurrying back from the doorway, with the deputy

122

marshal calling tersely to Matthew, 'He's on his way.'

'Get into the kitchen, woman,' Matthew ordered her, as he went to stand behind the desk, eyes going down to check that his Navy Colt was still in place. Then he picked up a pen, dipped it in an inkwell, and adopted an innocent pose by pretending to write.

A distraught Sadie ran to the kitchen. Foiled in her attempt to take Matthew's Colt, there was nothing she could do now to save Clancy. She couldn't blame herself for Oakes's intended action against the bogus US marshal, but she was solely responsible for Matthew's jealous crusade of vengeance. Clancy would be facing Oakes's rifle, not expecting a bullet from behind. It saddened her to realize that she had no need to ask herself if her husband was capable of shooting a man in the back: she fully accepted that he was.

Carefully and slowly, she closed the

kitchen door until there was a mini-
mum gap that allowed for a maximum
view. Through the narrow opening she
saw that Matthew had lighted a cigar
and blew out a puff of smoke as Barton
Clancy came up the steps and walked
into the hotel.

★   ★   ★

Though he gave the impression of
not anticipating any danger, Clancy's
senses were finely tuned as he walked
into the hotel lobby. A swift glance took
in Matthew Forston behind his desk,
with Tommy Oakes standing across the
room from him with his back to
the wall. Will Tarner was standing
casually in the dining-room doorway,
one heavily muscled shoulder resting
against the jamb. The door to the
kitchen was ajar, and through the
narrow gap Clancy caught a glimpse of
a white-faced Sadie Forston.

Raising his rifle to hip level, pointed
at Clancy, Oakes gave force to what he

124

said by spitting out the words. 'Take it slow, *Marshal*, and move over to stand by the desk.'

The way he laid emphasis on the word *Marshal* was a deliberate insult. Matthew Furston stopped writing and straightened up. Will Tarner still lounged against the door jamb, smiling a little now as he enjoyed the scene.

Remaining where he had stopped just inside of the door, a slightly mocking Clancy asked, 'Are you sure that you're up to this, boy?'

'Get over by the desk,' Oakes repeated his order, and Clancy noticed the second knuckle of his forefinger whiten as it tightened on the trigger of the rifle.

With no intention of putting himself in a vulnerable position, Clancy didn't move. Oakes gestured him toward the desk with a violent jerk of the rifle, but still Clancy stayed where he was.

The kitchen door opening took them all unawares. Sadie stepped out into the lobby, looking from one to the other of them before saying, 'Stop this, Matthew. Now!'

'Go back where you came from, woman,' Forston snarled.

'I will not,' Sadie replied defiantly. 'Stop this nonsense. Do you all want to be killed?'

'Ain't no call for anybody to be kilt, Miz Forston,' Tommy Oakes drawled. 'Not if Clancy here does what he's told. If he don't, then he'll be the only one what's kilt.'

Sadie's arrival in the lobby compromised Clancy's position. To ensure that she was out of the line of fire, he moved to the desk as Oakes had ordered. Though watching Oakes all the way, Clancy snatched a quick glance at Sadie. She gave him an almost imperceptible signal by moving her eyes to the left and down. He read the silent message and was grateful for it. Her husband had a gun under his desk.

With his back to the desk, Clancy spoke in a reasonable, close-to-friendly tone to Oakes. 'You got yourself a bit of a problem now, Tommy. Though you're ready to pull that trigger, you're wondering how fast I am. You're asking yourself, if you shoot will I be able to draw and drill you before I die. If I can, then you'll probably die, too. That is a sure enough nasty question. I know the answer to it, but you don't.'

The sudden doubt that showed clearly in Oakes's eyes rewarded Clancy. He saw the finger slacken on the trigger as the instinct of self-preservation tried to take over. If everything here had been fair, then the young deputy was already defeated. But Clancy saw Oakes's eyes go past him momentarily to look at Forston. Reassured by the hotelier's presence, the boy's nerves settled and his finger was again ready to squeeze the trigger.

Tension was building fast. Clancy relaxed his body in a special way that meant it could instantly explode into fast action. He was aware, however, that he was in a tight spot. Even as he heard Sadie's sharp intake of breath, he had already sensed that at his back Forston was bringing up his gun.

Sure of himself now, Tommy Oakes was grinning. Anticipation had Will Tarner straighten up in the doorway, a wide grin spreading over his big face. It had gone very quiet, without even the sound of a breath being taken by any of the four people in the lobby.

Then, although Matthew Forston was moving slowly so as to make no noise, the sound of him drawing back the hammer of his gun was very audible to Clancy.

6

Clancy's move was unexpected. Almost too fast for a human eye to follow, he stretched his right arm out and swung it behind him. It caught Forston in the face with a vicious, backhanded blow. The sound of the hotelier's cheekbone snapping was like a shot from a gun. Sent hurtling backwards, Forston's wail of agony disconcerted the inexperienced Oakes. Taking advantage of this, Clancy reached for and picked up the brass bell from the desk and threw it at the deputy marshal. The heavy bell caught Oakes on the left temple, splitting the skin above his eye. Blood gushed from the wound, stirring up an anger in Oakes which allowed him to regain control of himself. His mouth became lipless because they were rolled up against his yellow teeth. He brought the rifle back to bear on Clancy.

But Oakes had hesitated too long. Wanting to avoid gunplay because Sadie was there, Clancy was already leaping at him across the lobby. Grasping the barrel of the rifle with both hands, he wrenched the weapon from Oakes. Using the rifle like a battering ram, Clancy jabbed the deputy hard in the groin with the butt. Quick as a lightning flash, Clancy changed the rifle's use to that of a club as Oakes bent double, vomiting gushingly. Swinging the rifle sideways and upward, Clancy swiped the boy on the jaw with a force that straightened him up.

Oakes made a grotesque sight now as he stood, blank-eyed and swaying. The bottom half of his already bloodied face had been knocked to one side so that his jaw and mouth and chin was offset from the upper part of his head. Though he was out on his feet, something kept him standing. With a sideways kick of his right foot, Clancy caught him in the ankles, knocking his legs from under him.

As Oakes crashed to the floor, Will Tarner ran to him. Lying on his back, Oakes was making loud gurgling sounds as he choked on his own blood. Dropping to one knee, Tarner rolled his friend on to his side so that thick red blood spewed out on to the floor, partially clearing Oakes's airways as it did so. A concerned Tarner reached out with both hands and made an attempt at straightening Oakes's out-of-line face. But the pain he caused made Oakes release a shrill, piercing scream. It didn't seem possible that a human being could make such an eerie sound.

Unmoved by this drama, Clancy swung round to check on Matthew Forston. The hotelier was sitting where he had landed, his back propped against a wall. Holding his shattered face with both hands in an attempt at easing the pain, Forston was looking pleadingly at his wife for help. But Sadie stood motionless, looking down at him. She showed neither pity nor contempt for her husband. She just seemed completely bewildered, unable to understand what had happened.

Still holding Oakes's rifle, Clancy stooped to pick up from the floor the Navy Colt that Forston had intended to use. He tossed both weapons behind the counter and was turning toward Sadie when she cried out a warning.

With no time to react, Clancy saw Will Tarner's huge fist coming at him. The punch that caught him under the jaw was so powerful that it lifted him up off his feet. Sent flying over the desk, Clancy crashed against the wall before slumping to the floor.

Vaulting over the desk with an agility surprising in so big a man, Tarner landed in front of Clancy just as he was clawing at the wall to pull himself up. Tarner kneed him in the face. The back of his head cracking against the wall, Clancy was barely conscious. But he did see Tarner's booted foot aimed at his head. Able to move just far enough to one side, Clancy felt the wind of

Tarner's kick as it went by him to slam into the wall.

It was a close call that energized Clancy. Knowing that the huge blacksmith was capable of killing him with his bare hands, he rolled away to come up on to his knees. He was on his feet, swaying to avoid a punch from Tarner to his head. Clancy drove his own fist into his opponent's midriff, but Tarner's body was rock hard, and the beating Clancy had taken made his blow ineffective.

Unable to match Tarner in strength, Clancy knew that he would need to rely on speed. But his battered head still swam and consequently his reflexes were slowed. Dodging another punch, he picked up a chair by one leg and swung it at Tarner. Raising an arm to protect himself, the blacksmith's thick forearm splintered the chair into pieces.

Accepting that he was about to be beaten to a pulp, Clancy fought back desperately. Flicking Tarner across the eyes with the fingertips of his left hand, temporarily blinding him, Clancy released a right-hand punch that connected with the big man's jaw. The fact that his strength had been seriously depleted meant that Clancy's blow had only enough power to rock Tarner slightly.

With a mighty smash from a forearm, the blacksmith draped Clancy face down over the desk. Clutching his right shoulder, Tarner pulled Clancy round and got him by the throat with both hands. Powerful fingers closed off Clancy's windpipe.

Unlike taking blows with intervals between them, Clancy discovered that there was no respite in strangulation. Starved of air, his brain began playing tricks on him. For a moment he wasn't sure where he was or what was happening. Then Sadie's voice screaming at Tarner to stop brought Clancy back to reality.

But that reality lasted only a matter of seconds. Then consciousness started to fade fast and Clancy had the impression that he was spiralling down into a bottomless pit. He guessed morbidly that when he eventually landed he would be dead.

Then a single shot from a gun altered everything. The blacksmith's fingers released Clancy's throat. It seemed to Clancy that both he and his assailant had suddenly been caught in a severe hailstorm. He solved this mystery when, free of the weight of Tarner's body on him, he straightened up, holding his throat, coughing and gasping painfully for air.

Judge Keily stood just inside the entrance to the hotel, a smoking revolver in his hand. Clancy's mind cleared well enough to reason what had happened. Firing a shot to stop Tarner strangling Clancy, the judge's bullet had shattered the elegant chandelier that had graced the ceiling of the Rest and Welcome reception area. The hail failing on Clancy had been pieces of ornamental glass raining down.

'Stop this nonsense at once,' Judge Keily shouted at Tarner.

Recovering slowly, Clancy saw Keily scan the lobby, taking in everything. Though grateful for the judge's intervention, Clancy accepted that his pose as a US marshal was at an end. It was too soon to decide just what that would imply, but it meant certain trouble for him.

Throat aching, he looked to where Matthew Forston had got to his feet, still holding the side of his face. Sadie had moved away from her husband, keeping her eyes averted from everyone there. Will Tarner was helping Oakes into a chair. Nature seemed to have moved the deputy's jaw back into place, but the lower part of his face was hugely swollen and discoloured.

Clancy's eyes met those of the stern-faced judge, and he feared the worst.

★ ★ ★

The past hour had been a difficult one for Gilbert, but he had begun to hope that things would improve before long. Working with Nathan Powell in the yard at the rear of the jail, he had quickly realized that the local carpenter was totally incapable of grasping the concept of the innovative gallows. The principle of the windlass presented Nathan Powell with the most difficulty.

Even so, Powell was a fine craftsman who was worth cultivating. Discovering this had eased Gilbert's impatience, and now he was able to concentrate on watching and instructing the carpenter. Judge Keily having given his personal guarantee that Gilbert would receive his remarkably modest fee of one hundred dollars for the Paltroe execution had resolved the slight financial difficulty. By the end of that day, all being well, Gilbert would be in a position to assure the judge that his apparatus would be ready in time to accommodate Hank Paltroe in two mornings' time.

Gilbert admired the judge, and had gratefully accepted another invitation to dinner at his house that evening. That made him think of Clancy, who had also been invited. Would the fearless Clancy be there? Dire images of what might be happening at the hotel right then kept looming up in Gilbert's mind. Though if it came to it, he wouldn't be able to condone Clancy's deception, he was prepared to run with it providing that it didn't impinge on his business in Tularosa. The fact that Clancy had proved to be no threat to him when they had first met out in the wilds was sufficient to convince Gilbert that, though an outlaw, Clancy was not a bad man.

In fact, Gilbert liked Clancy and was glad that he was in Tularosa right then. Carrying out a hanging in his native New York never exposed Gilbert to serious danger, but the same couldn't be said for out West. Though Clancy wasn't a real marshal, he was a handy man to have around as a friend at a time like this in a town like this.

'It must be tough on him seeing us at work out here,' Powell remarked, breaking into Gilbert's thoughts.

'I don't understand, Mr Powell.'

Powell jerked his head toward the jail, saying, 'Him in there.'

Gilbert looked to a shadowy barred window. By screwing up his eyes, he could make out a dark face staring out. It disturbed him a little, as the condemned man's anguish watching the gallows being constructed would make Gilbert's job more difficult at the end. Gilbert had known for years that his was a divine calling in which he was entrusted to avoid the condemned ones suffering needless pain, and smooth their way out of this vale of tears by intoning a few well-timed words of fine sympathy. He truly believed that he had been called upon to emulate Jack Ketch, the historic hangman of Great Britain who was his idol.

Now that Hank Paltroe had traumatically viewed the building of the gallows, it would be more difficult for Gilbert, cometh the fateful hour, to calm him. But Gilbert was confident that he had the experience to cope and offer comfort to Paltroe before plunging him into the beyond.

'I've got a real bad feeling about this, Mr Gilbert,' Powell said, as he cut a joint more quickly and accurately than Gilbert had ever before witnessed. 'We ain't never had a hanging in Tularosa afore.'

'That's why you feel bad about it, Mr Powell. An execution brings a most unfortunate and gloomy atmosphere to a town. Even out here, on the Frontier, as it were, where folk have become accustomed to sudden and violent death, the deaths of those who live and die by the gun are not premeditated. It is a very different matter when a man is locked away to be led out at a predetermined time and put to death.'

Agreeing with a hesitant nod, Powell said, 'I suppose that's it. But there's something else, some other feeling I have that — '

The carpenter broke off speaking as the sound of a single shot reached them. It had come from afar, but not from too great a distance. Aware that the most likely location was the Rest and Welcome Hotel, Gilbert quickly put down the measuring stick he was holding.

'I have to leave you to it,' he told a bemused Nathan Powell as he dashed out of the yard.

★   ★   ★

'It suits you,' Hilda Stewart simpered.

Holding the pale-blue dress up against her, Cora Caddo thought wryly how the two church-going Miss Stewarts regarded her as immoral yet found her money to be perfectly acceptable. Studying her reflection in the shop's full-length mirror, she liked the way the dress hung straight down before being gradually widened at the waist by crinolines. It would cost her two weeks' pay, but it was worth it. She imagined the marshal seeing her in the dress for the first time. Anticipation of that thrilling moment persuaded her that she had to have the dress at any cost. Wise in the ways of men, Cora had been delighted to notice that Ronan Lombard was far from immune to her charms. One day soon he would be riding out of Tularosa, and Cora was determined to do everything possible to ensure that she would leave with him.

'I do like it,' she said to the spinster shopkeeper.

'You couldn't make a better choice.' Hilda Stewart applied a little sales pressure as she glanced curiously at her sister.

Emily Stewart was standing looking out of the window, the tip of her long beak of a nose touching the glass. She spoke without turning her head. 'I'm sure that there's something going on in the Rest and Welcome, Hilda. Tommy Oakes went in there earlier, carrying a rifle. Madge Keily's young man was with him. A little while ago, that marshal fellow walked over to the hotel. Something about him made me nervous. I noticed that he drew his gun and sort of checked it before he went in.'

Hearing this worried Cora. She was sure that Tommy Oakes was scheming to do Ronan Lombard harm, and feared that whatever it was could be about to happen. A pang of conscience tormented her as she realized that her anxiety was not for Oakes, a boyfriend of sorts for some time, but the US marshal, a newcomer to Tularosa.

'It wouldn't surprise me if it was some kind of argument over Sadie Forston,' Hilda Stewart commented. 'She's no better than she ought to be.'

'For all her airs and graces, I always had her down as a dancehall girl,' Emily Stewart sniffed, from her position at the window.'

'And we know what *they* are,' Hilda said contemptuously. Then her thin, wrinkled-skin face reddened as she remembered Cora's presence, and also recalled that the deal on the blue dress had not been finalized. She forced a smile. 'Present company excepted, of course.'

'Of course,' Cora replied, conscious that she was being just as false as the dried-up old woman, but not caring because she had to have the dress.

There could be a lot of truth in Emily Stewart's opinion of Sadie Forston. Cora remembered drinking with a gun salesman who had boarded at the Rest and Welcome while in Tularosa. He had been pretty certain that he had seen Sadie working in a saloon in a cow town down south. Because she wasn't in a position to pass judgment on any woman, Cora had paid little attention at the time. But she had been jealous of Sadie Forston ever since the US marshal had been staying at the hotel, and the spinster's remark about men arguing over the hotel woman had fanned the flames of that jealousy.

'I don't know why Will Tarner would want to get involved with the Forston woman,' Hilda said indignantly. 'He must realize how lucky he is to have a wonderful girl like Madge.'

'Perhaps that lad Oakes has set his cap at the Forston woman and, being his friend, Tarner has gone along to support him,' Emily suggested, with a spinster's logic. 'If Sadie Forston has a thing going with that marshal fellow, then young Oakes would be foolish to go up against such a man. Just seeing him on the street simply terrifies me.'

Hearing this conversation relieved Cora. Sadie Forston would be interested in Ronan Lombard, as would most women, but the hotel woman would not give a boy like Tommy Oakes a second glance. But the feeling of relief faded rapidly when Cora considered the alternative. Whatever was happening at the hotel had to be to do with Tommy Oakes's obvious determination to rid Tularosa of Ronan Lombard.

Still holding the dress against her, she took another look in the mirror while trying to dream up an excuse to go over to the hotel. Sure of a sale now, Hilda

Stewart was smiling at her indulgently when the sharp bark of a gun being fired alarmed all three of them.

'I knew it,' Emily cried out triumphantly. 'That shot came from the Rest and Welcome.'

The smile fell from Hilda Stewart's face and she watched, agape and speechless, as Cora dropped the expensive dress carelessly on the counter and rushed from the shop. Hilda went to the window to stand beside her sister. Together they watched Cora Caddo run toward the Rest and Welcome Hotel.

★ ★ ★

'I warned you about starting something like this, Oakes,' Judge Keily thundered, pointing an accusing finger at the deputy marshal.

Sitting in the chair, held in an upright position by Tarner, Oakes tried to reply. But his broken jaw wouldn't work, and the effort plainly caused him immense pain. Blood from the cut above it filled one of his eyes, and tears welled up in the other. Watching the tears spill out to run down a damaged cheek, Clancy felt remorse. Oakes was little more than a boy, and he was racked by guilt at having given him such a thrashing. But he took consolation in the knowledge that Oakes had acted like a man, and had forced the confrontation. The boy had probably learned a valuable lesson, that no one should ever start something they couldn't finish.

Somehow managing to speak, Oakes's words were slurred by grossly swollen lips. 'I had to act, Judge. That man is an impostor. I reckon he's here to break Poltroe out of jail. His real name is Barton Clancy, and he's an outlaw who's wanted in Sante Fe for murder.'

'That's preposterous,' the judge snorted. He pointed to Clancy's holstered Colt .45. 'Though it is obvious that you threatened him with a rifle, Marshal Lombard did not even attempt to draw his gun. Is that how you'd expect an outlaw, a man wanted for murder, to act?'

Watching Oakes, impeded by a slow brain and a damaged mouth, unable to answer, and finding it difficult to believe his luck in having Judge Keily support him, Clancy had another surprise as an agitated Gilbert came bursting into the hotel.

The hangman wore his habitual frown as he spoke to the judge. 'Forgive me should I be transgressing, Judge Keily, but is my understanding of this situation correct? Are Marshal Lombard's credentials being questioned?'

'Oakes has seen fit to question his very identity,' the judge replied.

Baffled by Gilbert's arrival and intercession, Clancy tried, but failed, to guess what the hangman's purpose was. Although he had agreed not to expose Clancy as a fraud, Gilbert had done so benignly. But now the hangman was playing an active role in protecting him.

'That is absolutely absurd, Judge Keily,' Gilbert strongly protested. 'As I was uncertain at the time, I didn't mention it when you introduced me to the marshal at your house. But I had this inkling, as one does, that I had met Marshal Lombard before. I realized a little later that we had indeed met, albeit briefly. Many months ago my services were required in El Paso. US Marshal Ronan Lombard apprehended the unfortunate condemned one, and he attended the execution. At the . . . ah . . . ceremony, so to speak, I saw US Marshal Lombard was in the company of the State Governor.'

A satisfied smile twitching at the corners of his mouth, Judge Keily asked, 'And that man you saw in El Paso is the man standing here with us at this very moment, the man we know as US Marshal Ronan Lombard?'

'One and the same,' Gilbert emphatically confirmed.

'There was a reward notice with Clancy's picture on it in Abel Turner's desk.' Oakes, now extremely distressed physically, managed to mumble.

'The dodger that wasn't there when

you tried to show it to me,' the judge commented sarcastically.

'I find the very suggestion ludicrous,' Gilbert said with a slow, disbelieving shake of his head. 'There is no shadow of a doubt in my mind that this is US Marshal Ronan Lombard.'

'Then that is good enough for me,' Judge Keily said, turning his head to look as Cora Caddo stepped hesitantly into the hotel.

'Ask her,' Tommy Oakes shouted, immediately suffering for the effort required. On the verge of collapsing, it needed all of Tarner's strength to hold him upright on the chair. 'She was in the office when I found the dodger, and she must have taken it when I'd left.'

'What do you have to say in answer to that, Cora?' the judge asked.

Looking around her, confused and afraid, the saloon girl's gaze remained on Clancy. Her eyes implored him to help her. To offer her some way out of her bewilderment as everyone there stared at her, waiting, for an answer.

But there was nothing Clancy could do. If she had stolen the dodger to protect him, then he probably owed her his life. But, having just escaped detection by the skin of his teeth, there was no way to repay her at that moment.

'Did you take the reward notice, girl?' the judge questioned her relentlessly.

Shaking her head, Cora answered in a hoarse whisper, 'I know nothing about any notice, sir.'

'I believe you, child.' The judge gave an emphatic nod and glared round at all present. 'Let this be an end to it.' He walked over to Clancy, his right hand extended. 'I know that you are a big enough man, Marshal Lombard, to accept my apologies on behalf of the people of Tularosa for this unfortunate incident.'

'Of course, sir,' Clancy responded, shaking the judge by the hand. 'I'm real thankful that nobody got hurt.'

As Clancy's sentence ended there came an almighty crash. An unconscious Tommy Oakes had pitched forward head first from his chair on to the floor. Clancy was sure that the irony of this happening at the time of his remark about nobody having been hurt, brought a twinkle of amusement to Keily's eyes.

Quickly resuming his customary officious manner, the judge turned to the saloon girl. 'Please fetch Doc Hartley as quick as you can, Cora. We need to get Oakes fixed up, and Matthew will need to have his face looked at. Are you feeling all right, Marshal?'

'I feel great, Judge,' Clancy truthfully replied.

7

As the last ray of sunlight had been dragged over the horizon, a slight breeze replaced it. Cool, purple shadows had crept far out across the flat, and the dark green of the foothills became almost black as Madge Keily and Clancy sat on the veranda of the judge's house. Most of the time the moon was hidden behind trees, but it was a full moon and there was ample light to accentuate the intelligent features of Madge's intensely alive face. Clancy sensed something magic in the silence that was night.

It had been a pleasant evening. Clancy had enjoyed it so much that he deeply regretted being a guest of the Keilys under false pretences. Had it been for real, then sitting out here in the night with Madge would have been even more special. No real relationship can be built on a lie. A few hours spent living the way most people did made him realize how much of his life had been spent in hiding while planning a robbery, or on the run after carrying out a robbery. Being with Madge Keily made him want things to be different.

Over dinner, the judge had been embarrassingly obvious in his attempts to bring his daughter and Clancy closer together. There had been no mention of the altercation at the hotel, and Will Tarner was absent. The Keilys had tacitly let Claney know that the blacksmith was unwelcome and had not been invited to dinner. He guessed that this was because although Matthew Forston had grudgingly apologized to Clancy for what he termed a 'misunderstanding', and had assured him that he was welcome to stay on in his room at the hotel, Tarner had said nothing. Instead, the blacksmith had persisted in glowering threateningly at Clancy. The young giant had a grievance that he would want to settle. Clancy was glad that it wasn't this evening.

'I like Gilbert,' Madge said unexpectedly, her rapt appreciation of the glory of the night seeming to be suddenly broken. 'He is a superb conversationalist, but I find it impossible to accept his profession. I just can't imagine so mild and likeable a man as Gilbert being a hangman.'

'I think he sees himself as a saviour rather than an executioner,' Clancy said in defence of the man who had so stoically befriended him. 'The way he looks at it is that he has no way of preventing the law from hanging people, so it is up to him to make sure that those being hanged suffer as little as possible.'

'That makes me feel easier about him, Ronan,' Madge said, and it hurt Clancy to hear her call him by a name that wasn't his. He felt a sudden urge to blurt out the truth about himself. He was stopped by the thought of how disastrous that would be. She continued, 'Gilbert is obviously a kind man, though dedicated to his work.'

He certainly was dedicated, Clancy agreed silently, remembering one of the stories the profoundly serious but nevertheless entertaining hangman had regaled them with earlier in the evening. 'I will never forget 13 July 1860,' Gilbert had told them in his intense way of speaking. 'I suppose that it was the biggest day of my life. It was on Bedloe's Island, New York, where I had been called to mete out the penalty of the law on one Alfred E. Hicks, an especially brutal robber and murderer. There was massive interest in the execution of this notorious man and, at the risk of being immodest, in my innovative apparatus. Water carriers by the hundreds, private and excursion, all heavily loaded with people, hugged the island shore. The *Great Eastern*, having recently arrived on her first voyage to this country, lay at the foot of Hammond Street. There was a crowd of an estimated ten thousand spectators, and the pier was lined by a platoon of marines under the command of Captain John B. Hall. They paraded with the troops from Fort Hamilton and Governors Island, and then all of them marched to form a square around the scaffold which I had erected within twenty feet of the shore.'

'This Hicks must have been very famous,' Judge Keily, caught up in the story as was everyone else, had commented.

'Infamous, Judge, infamous,' Gilbert had explained, 'though I would never deny any man credit for bravery, and Hicks was a most courageous man. Immediately on landing on the island he knelt down and prayed silently for a few moments, and then proceeded to the scaffold with his head high. Hicks was executed at precisely five minutes past eleven.'

'I imagine that the man's grave must have become some sort of shrine, Mr Gilbert.' Gwendoline Keily had suggested when Gilbert's tale ended.

'Strangely not, Mrs Keily.' The frown

Gilbert wore like a trademark had deepened when he replied. 'The body was placed in a coffin and buried in Calvary Cemetery. No stone was ever erected to show the precise spot, which was as well because of what transpired. Forgive this macabre twist at the dinner-table, ladies, but the corpse was removed a night or two after the burial by some body-snatchers and sold for dissection.'

Now, as if reading Clancy's thoughts, Madge said, 'That was an horrific story about the man named Hicks, but I must confess that I was enthralled by Gilbert's talent at story-telling.

'He was talking on his favourite subject, Madge,' Clancy smiled. 'By all accounts Gilbert is not just the hangman at executions, he takes over completely as the master of ceremonies.'

'I can imagine that,' Madge said with a little laugh. 'Yet though I have learnt to like Gilbert, Ronan, I will be glad when the day after tomorrow has come and gone, and this Paltroe business has ended. It's a black cloud hanging over our town.' She added quietly and shyly, 'But I will have one regret.'

'What is that?' an unsuspecting Clancy enquired.

A few moments went by before Madge answered. 'That your job here will be at an end. Duty will call and you will leave Tularosa.'

Smothering a mixture of embarrassment and excitement, she surveyed him covertly. A breeze stirred lazily and for a second Clancy caught the scent of her hair through the waft of perfume from the quiet night flowers in the garden. Though he felt the same way she did, as Ronan Lombard it wasn't possible for him to give the response that Madge was clearly expecting. As Barton Clancy he would have had no problem advancing their relationship. But Clancy would not be sitting with a judge's daughter on the veranda of the judge's house. Clancy remained silent.

'There was something that I meant to

mention to you,' Madge began, disappointment evident in her tone. 'A stranger came into the bank today making enquiries.'

'You think that he may have been one of the Paltroe gang?' Clancy asked, suddenly apprehensive.

Madge gave a slow, doubtful shake of her head. 'I wouldn't think so. He said he was a cattle-buyer looking for stock. Norman, Mr Spelling that is, suggested that he ride out to the Lazy L and speak to Geoff Arthur.'

'That was all?' Clancy checked. 'He took no interest in the bank itself?'

'Not particularly, Ronan. He did ask a few questions in case, as he said, he should do a lot of business in the area.'

'Was this man wearing a gun, Madge?'

'Oh no. He was dressed like and had the manners of a gentleman.'

'What did he look like?' Clancy questioned her, trying to sound casual.

'I would say he was around forty, not particularly tall. His hair was dark, perhaps black, and when he took off his hat I noticed a scar running up from his forehead into his hair.'

'You should have been a law officer, Madge,' Clancy said jokingly, in praise of her powers of observation.

He had spoken mildly and in jest, but a sudden bitterness swept over him. Madge Keily had just described Josie Paltroe. Both of the Paltroe brothers could present themselves to the world as gentlemen when it suited them. Josie had visited Tularosa to size up the bank and the jail.

Learning this, Clancy knew that the day after tomorrow would not be going the way he had planned. There was big trouble ahead.

★　★　★

From across open prairie, Reb Hawker and Ike Short approached the trail into Tularosa. The hour was late and the moonlit night very still. Protected by the shoulder of a little knoll, they pulled up their horses.

161

'We'll wait here for him,' Ike Short said 'He oughta be along in ten, fifteen minutes.'

The hard-faced Reb Hawker said nothing. Short knew him well enough not to have expected him to speak. Staying in the saddle their alert eyes fastened on the trail that in the moonlight they could see twisting over the flat, treeless plain like a silvery ribbon.

– The minutes dragged by with only the chomping of their horses breaking the stillness of the night. Both men were by nature followers and not leaders. Neither of them liked the period of uncertainty that Josie Paltroe was putting them through. The fact that Paltroe was reconnoitring the town and that two of the old gang, the knifeman Bill Coffey and fast-gun Luke Sontag, were to join them in the morning, made it evident that Paltroe didn't intend doing it Clancy's way, the easy way, the best way.

Taking the makings from the top

pocket of his jacket, Ike Short rolled a cigarette. Watching him, Hawker spoke sharply. 'If you got to smoke, then get down out of the saddle and hug the ground. We're in unknown territory here.'

Instead of reaching for a match, Short put the unlit cigarette into the same pocket as the makings. He recognized that Hawker was right. He hadn't been thinking properly, but he wasn't about to admit that to his taciturn companion. He tightened the reins of the saddled horse he was leading. The stirrups had been draped over the horn to prevent them from flapping against the horse's sides should something unexpected mean that they had to leave in a hurry. The spare horse had been brought along in case Josie Paltroe ran into trouble and needed it. That was one of the emergency contingencies that Clancy had introduced to the gang, and all of them had faithfully followed it ever since.

'I don't like it,' Short groaned.

'Something must have happened to him. It ain't like Josie to keep us waiting. If Josie's in trouble we should be riding in now to help him.'

'Settle down,' Hawker advised gruffly. 'There's someone coming now. Who else but Paltroe would be out here in this barren land at gone midnight?'

They waited three or four minutes as the horseman drew nearer. He was riding an easily identified long-legged sorrel.

'That's Josie, sure enough,' Ike Short declared with relief. 'We can ride down to the trail.'

Paltroe saw them coming and let the sorrel amble along at an even pace. Dressed in gentleman's clothes, he looked tired but relaxed.

'You look like a preacher. Josie,' Ike Short chuckled. 'There ain't a sheriff in the land who would know you in that get-up. We were afeared that you'd got catched in town.'

Paltroe said. 'All went well. They plan on stringing Hank up tomorrow morning.'

164

'Tomorrow morning?' Short croaked. 'That only gives a few hours, Josie.'

'It's already today, Ike,' Hawker said, in a voice that was rusty from disuse. 'Tomorrow morning means *tomorrow* morning.'

Agreeing, Paltroe looked pleased with himself. 'That's right. Bill and Luke will be here by then. That town is a sitting duck, boys.'

'Clancy said they had the streets covered by rifles,' Ike Short said nervously.

'Barton Clancy ain't the man he used to be, Ike,' Paltroe said, knuckling his tired eyes. 'It's getting so bad that he's sometimes scared of shadows. There ain't nothing in Tularosa to worry us. I've had me a good looksee.'

'We get Hank out and knock over the bank?' Hawker asked, in what was a long speech by his standards.

'We do.'

'Hank first, then the bank, Josie?' Short asked.

'No,' Paltroe shook his head. 'The

bank's easy. There's only an excuse for a man and a girl working there. And here's the good bit. The girl is the daughter of Judge Keily, the old *hombre* who runs the town. We hit the bank and take the girl. Then we do a trade, the judge's daughter in exchange for Hank.'

'That's a good 'un, Josie,' Ike Short chortled.

'What about Clancy?' Hawker asked.

'What about Clancy?' Paltroe returned the question he had been asked. 'I guess Clancy's come to a fork in the trail, Reb. He's kind of real settled in town, and I ain't sure which way he'll run when the lead starts to fly.'

'I reckon as how Clancy's always been one of us, and he'll be with us in Tularosa,' Short said hopefully.

Reb Hawker gave his opinion. 'He's a good man to have around, Josie, and we need him.'

'Time will tell,' Paltroe said, obviously annoyed by the faith expressed in Clancy. 'But, with or without Clancy, we got things to do in Tularosa that need planning. So let's head back for camp to get some shut-eye, then we'll work out just how we're going to do it.'

Paltroe jabbed the flanks of his horse and moved off. Not moving their horses for a moment, Hawker and Short exchanged worried glances. Then, with a resigned sigh from Ike Short, they reined about and rode off behind Josie Paltroe.

★   ★   ★

The pleasant evening spent at the Keily home had ended. But as Clancy made his way through the deserted town to the hotel, the warmth and thrill of being with Madge had stayed with him. But the glow faded fast as he made his way through a shadowy yard in which Tularosa's grain merchant and haulier marshalled their wagons. He felt a certainty that something was about to happen. The very quiet that hugged the night air gave fair warning of it to

Clancy. The spell of rigid quiet held him tighter as he walked further into the yard and the surrounding buildings cut off the moonlight. Clancy instinctively eased his six-shooter in its holster.

Six feet ahead of him the shadow of a wagon changed shape slightly. Someone lurking there had moved. Drawing his gun, Clancy let it slide back into the holster as the massive figure of Will Tarner stepped out in front of him. The blacksmith wouldn't be armed. Most young pretenders made a fast-draw challenge, but with Tarner it would be fists.

'Had a nice evening, Clancy?'

He was no more than a silhouette to Clancy, but the sneer in Tarner's tone was unmistakable.

'The name's Lombard. US Marshal Lombard, and I had a real good evening.'

'The good times end here, Clancy,' Tarner said with a rumbling chuckle. 'To reach the Rest and Welcome you've got to get past me.'

Tarner stood there, supremely confident. Broad-shouldered and deep-chested, he was a giant who had never known the limit of his own strength, and was likely the most dangerous unarmed man within a hundred-mile circle. Clancy's guess was that young blacksmith must weigh at least 260 pounds. No matter who emerged as victor, Clancy accepted that they would both be badly hurt.

'I don't see any real problem in getting past you, Tarner,' Clancy said, in a quiet voice.

'I don't reckon as how you do, seeing as I ain't carrying a gun and you are,' the blacksmith nodded. 'But a fast draw don't make you a real man. The way I see it, the only way to do that is with your fists.'

'In this case, I agree with you,' Clancy said mildly.

'How do I know that you won't draw that gun when I'm giving you a walloping?'

Making a show of it not being a

threat, Clancy used a finger and a thumb to draw his .45 and lay it on a flat cart that stood a few feet away. He assured Tarner, 'My gun will be out of reach.'

Clancy was turning back to Tarner when the blacksmith's powerful right hand swung out. In a lightning move, the intention was to grasp Clancy's collar and pull him on to what would have been a crushing uppercut from Tarner's left hand. But the blacksmith's right hand didn't reach its target. Instead, the towering man-mountain was carried backward by a right hook delivered with striking-rattler swiftness to his jaw. The punch had the lifting force of a kicking mule, and it drove Tarner's head back, stretching his neck muscles to the limit. Using some neat footwork, Clancy set himself up to slam another terrific blow that exploded hard and flat against the broad point of the blacksmith's chin. Aware that it would be a battle of speed versus brute strength, Clancy couldn't believe how easy it was. Tarner had raised his arms to protect his face, so Clancy attacked the big body. Sinking a left-hand punch in deep, he delivered a one-two with his right hand; one punch landing under the heart, the other above it. Energy sapping blows.

Encouraged by the fact that the big man didn't lower his arms, Clancy sent a barrage of blows to the body, left and right, left and right, aware of the effect it was having on Tarner by the way he grunted gaspingly and his body reacted. But finding the blacksmith so easy a target lured Clancy into over-confidence.

Withstanding the battering his body was taking, Tarner raised both of his massive arms above his head. Lacing his fingers together, he brought both hands crashing down on the top of Clancy's head.

Feeling as if his neck had been driven down into his body, Clancy reeled back. Lashing out with his right foot from where he stood, the blacksmith caught Clancy under the left knee with a kick from his heavy boot. Pain from the kick racking his whole body, Clancy fell forward. Now it was Tarner's turn to show a blinding speed. Pivoting on his left foot, he back-heeled the falling Clancy under the chin.

Knocked unconscious momentarily, Clancy came round as his back crashed painfully against a wagon. Grasping a wheel with both hands saved him from going down. But Tarner was rushing at him, head down like a charging bull. Struggling to put together the shattered bits of his fighting mind, Clancy regained much of his ability. Intent on driving his head hard into the stomach of his motionless, helpless victim, Tarner came rushing on.

Timing it precisely, Clancy didn't move until the blacksmith's head was only inches from him. Gaining leverage from his grip on the wheel, Clancy pulled himself sideways at the last second. Caught unawares, Tarner couldn't prevent his head colliding against the wheel with stunning force.

Still holding on to the wheel, Clancy brought his knee up hard into the blacksmith's ribs before the shaken big man could straighten up. Knocked sideways, Tarner went down on one knee. Still badly hurt, Clancy clung on to the wheel and kicked out with his right foot. The toe of his boot caught Tarner on the bridge of his nose, messily smashing it and knocking him flat on his back.

Disadvantaged in both weight and size, Clancy knew that no rules could apply in this fight. Jumping to land lightly by the prone blacksmith, he dropped so that one of his knees was on the barrel chest, while he pressed the other knee down hard on Tarner's throat, crushing his windpipe.

Gasping and choking, Tarner lay threshing his arms about on each side of him as he fought for breath. Clancy was digging his knee in for the kill when he learned that he had underestimated the blacksmith's strength. Tarner arched his body up, first unbalancing

Clancy, before reaching up with both hands he gripped Clancy's right thigh and right upper arm. Without effort, he threw him.

Doing an involuntary somersault, Clancy hit the ground in a bone-jarring crash. He saw that Tarner had already gained his feet and was coming at him. Having managed to only get up to a crouching position, Clancy felt himself grabbed again by the right leg and arm. With unbelievable strength and an animal-like roar, the blacksmith then straightened up. Then he raised Clancy above his head with both arms. Locking his elbows, Tarner then sent Clancy flying through the air with a tremendous throw.

Landing agonizingly with his back across the shaft of a wagon. Clancy rolled to the ground and came instantly up on to his knees. Tarner was coming in to finish him, but the pain Clancy was suffering somehow served to clear his head and bring his natural fighting self into play.

Up on his feet, Clancy faced Tarner. With a fast weaving and bobbing, and darting from side to side, his body seemed as supple as rubber. Tarner was watching his movements, trying to get in with a blow, but Clancy was now living up to the reputation he had gained throughout the West.

Two vicious blows, a right and a left, caught the blacksmith and reeled him backward. In a cold, calculating rage, Clancy went after him, closing in to deliver a right hook flush on the giant's mouth. His lips mashed and ripped to shreds against his teeth. Tarner whimpered like a child.

But he didn't go down. Somehow he remained standing on legs that, though as thick as tree trunks, were trembling. The merciless Clancy moved in on him again. Another right deliberately aimed at the blacksmith's bleeding ruin of a mouth, landed right on target. In a split second a right from Clancy had Tarner do a quarter turn.

Unable to face more punishment,

Tarner staggered off into the darkness like a wounded animal. Clancy started after him. But the world suddenly began turning, slow at first and then spinning to rob him of his balance. Battered and exhausted, he dropped to the ground, unconscious.

Clancy was brought back to consciousness by something wet, rough, and unpleasant wiping across his face. Head aching abysmally, he forced his eyes open one at a time. He was lying on the ground and a yellow cur was zealously licking his face.

Then Cora Caddo was leaning over him, peering through the poor light to exclaim, '*Madre de Dios*. What happened to you?'

'You should see the other fellow,' Clancy joked weakly, as she gently helped him up from the ground.

'I've heard that one a few times.'

'This time it's true,' Clancy mumbled, unashamedly leaning on the girl to support himself.

Tenderly wiping his bleeding face

176

with a dainty lace handkerchief, she said, 'I find it easy to believe that. Come on. If we take it slowly I'll get you back to the hotel. Put your arm around my shoulders.'

8

'I've strapped up his ribs and done what I can for his back.' Sitting on the edge of the hotel bed putting the finishing touches to bandaging Clancy's chest, Doc Hartley turned his head, speaking over his shoulder to Judge Keily. 'In four or five days' time he'll be as right as rain.'

Standing impatiently by the door, the judge replied anxiously, 'We don't have four or five days. You sure that you're right, Doc?'

Hartley, a slender, pleasant-faced boy with a bright red spot on both cheeks and hair that just missed being curly, stood up from the bed and looked at Keily with eyes that were infinitely old and weary. 'I graduated in medicine, Judge, musty, boring stuff.'

'I'm not questioning your qualifications, Doc,' the judge said swiftly and apologetically. 'It's just this diagnosis that worries me.'

'Maybe I'm wrong.' Hartley shrugged his narrow shoulders. 'I came out West in the hope the air will cure my chest. The fact that I can't heal myself shows how limited a physician's skills are.'

Keily raised both hands in a placating gesture. 'You've made a good name for yourself here in Tularosa, Doc, and I'd never be critical. It's just that this town can't afford to have Marshal Lombard out of action for that long.'

'Perhaps it won't take that long,' Hartley said, glancing to where Cora Caddo was fussing over the patient. Looking out of place in a low-cut blue dress, the saloon girl's efficient manner left no doubt that she cared deeply about her patient. Curled up asleep on the floor not far from her was Cora's constant companion, the yellow cur. The doctor smiled a little tired smile, and shook his head. 'The dog may not be suitable for a sick-room, but the marshal has a dedicated nurse. With luck he could be up and about in two to three days.'

'Not soon enough,' the judge sighed. 'The hanging takes place tomorrow morning.'

'Then Marshal Lombard won't be there,' Doc Hartley said emphatically.

★ ★ ★

Dismounting with difficulty at the creek, Will Tarner staggered two or three steps forward to drop to his knees at the water's edge. Every inch of his body hurt, his mashed lips felt as if they were on fire, and he couldn't breathe through his flattened nose. Eagerly scooping up the cold water with both hands, he splashed it on his face. First contact with the water was so torturous that he almost cried out in agony. Then the coldness became soothing. Bathing his face again, he carefully explored the damage with his fingertips. His lips felt swollen to four times their size. The bridge of his nose was broken, and though it was too sore to probe, Tarner realized that what had partially blocked the vision of his right eye was a jagged piece of nose-bone protruding through the skin.

The water had settled to a mirror surface and he recoiled on seeing his reflection. It bore no resemblance to his face. In fact it didn't look anything like a face. Seeing himself made Tarner glad that he had decided to ride out of Tularosa right after having escaped from Clancey's punishing fists. He couldn't have allowed anyone in town to see him in this state. Though his worth as a blacksmith was appreciated, he was best known for his physical prowess. He was feared by men and idolized by boys.

Now Clancy had deprived him of that recognition. What he regretted most of all was leaving Madge Keily. Skulking away from her like a whipped dog. The shame of it was becoming unbearable. Without any real plan for the future right then, he knew that he was young enough and strong enough to start over again in some other town. But he would never find a girl who meant so much to him as Madge did. That knowledge increased the hatred he felt for Clancy.

Summoning up the nerve to sneak another look at himself, he stiffened in apprehension on seeing the reflection of a pair of legs in ornamental high-heeled boots standing behind him. At the same time, Tarner felt the hard muzzle of a six-shooter press against the back of his head. A voice spoke to him in a surprisingly friendly way.

'You look like a man who's just had more than his fair share of trouble, *amigo*, so you won't be looking for more. Stand up real careful, stranger, and turned around.'

Obeying, Tarner found that his body was every bit as painful as before. But his face felt a little easier. On his feet, his head swimming a little, he turned to see five men, all of them with the look of desperadoes. The gun that had been pressed against his head was now held hip high, aiming at him. The leader, the man holding the gun, obviously satisfied by a glance that Tarner was unarmed, reholstered the weapon.

Sure that this was the famed Paltroe gang, Tarner experienced a fear that could escalate to terror at any moment.

'Are you from Tularosa?' the gang leader asked.

Tarner nodded, and another man, who wore a perpetual smile on his face, commented, 'You look like you tangled with a mountain lion, feller.'

The leader stepped closer to Tarner, surveying his face, inspecting the cuts and bruises. He shook his head. 'Not a mountain lion, Ike. I'd say that our new friend has had a run-in with a *mal hombre* named Clancy.' He looked questioningly at Tarner. 'Maybe you know him as US Marshal Ronan Lombard?'

'I know him by both names,' Tarner answered bitterly.

'So, now you're heading out of

Tularosa,' the gang leader remarked, with a sad shake of his head. 'Big mistake. It's a mistake to run away from Barton Clancy. No man has ever been able to run fast enough or far enough.'

With a grimace that spread agony through his battered face, Tarner complained, 'I ain't running away from Clancy. There's nothing left for me in Tularosa.'

'Because of Clancy,' the leader said. 'Well, it's lucky you met up with us, *mi amigo*. I'm Josie Paltroe, a man with a real grievance against your town. Me'n' the boys will be riding in there soon to put right what's been done to us. I'd be right happy to take you along with us, giving you the chance to get even with Barton Clancy and Tularosa. You interested?'

The idea held an appeal for Tarner, although he feared what might be involved in the offer. But he hadn't liked the idea of fleeing Tularosa after taking a beating. What Paltroe was offering meant that Madge Keily wouldn't be lost to him. But at what price? These men were outlaws. Tarner was well aware that he wasn't of their ilk and that to join up with them could prove to be disastrous. Josie Paltroe plainly had a use for him in mind, and it doubtless wouldn't be something Tarner would welcome. But he had no choice. If he refused he would most likely be gunned down where he stood.

'I'm interested,' Tarner heard himself say.

★ ★ ★

As Gilbert entered the jail office, Judge Keily, who was in the late Abel Turner's chair behind the late town marshal's desk, gestured for him to take a seat. Tommy Oakes, having physically recovered from Clancy's rough treatment, balanced on one buttock on the edge of the desk. Looking perplexed, apprehensive, Gilbert sat against a wall, facing them.

'We have a problem, Gilbert,' the judge said.

A nervous affliction causing him to stretch his chin up, freeing his neck from his shirt collar, Gilbert said unhappily, 'As an artist who ensures that there will be no complications in his work, Judge Keily, I must say that I won't tolerate problems created by others.'

'I appreciate that, Gilbert, of course I do,' the judge said. 'But in mitigation I would stress that this problem is not of my making. You will have heard that Marshal Lombard is indisposed.'

'Indeed I have, Judge. The disturbing news reached me first thing this morning. As I consider the marshal to be a friend, a very good friend, I visited him in his room at the hotel. Plainly, Judge, Marshal Lombard has been the victim of a most violent assault.'

'Having got to know the marshal, Gilbert,' the judge said, a smile playing at the corners of his mouth, 'I would say that he would have given as good as he got, probably better.'

Accepting this, Gilbert said, 'Indeed,

Marshal Lombard is truly a remarkable man, but it did distress me to see how bad his condition is.'

'I agree, it is most unfortunate,' Keily said sadly. 'Another cause for regret is the fact that it will be several days before the marshal will be fit. Which brings me to why I asked you to come here, Gilbert. The town will pay you extra, that goes without saying, if you could set the execution back, shall we say . . . three days?'

'For what reason, Judge Keily?'

Exasperated at being asked a question to which the answer was glaringly obvious, the judge couldn't prevent his irritation from being revealed in his voice. 'The reason is your safety and the safety of everyone in this town, Gilbert. With Marshal Lombard on duty the hanging of Hank Paltroe will go smoothly. But with the marshal on his sick bed, Tularosa will most probably be subjected to mayhem and murder. In addition, Paltroe is likely to be rescued and escape the gallows.'

Head nodding, Gilbert concurred. 'I understand what you are saying, Judge. We could indeed find ourselves faced with a deplorable situation.'

'So, you will postpone the hanging?'

'After clarifying one point,' Gilbert answered, holding one hand aloft to stay any further words from Keily. 'That is, has the condemned one been informed that he faces the gallows tomorrow morning?'

'He has,' the judge confirmed, 'but I can immediately send Deputy Town Marshal Oakes to him to explain the delay.'

Tommy Oakes had slid off the desk and was walking to the door when Gilbert jumped to his feet, his normally low voice raised to a one-word shout. 'NO!'

'With respect, Gilbert. I consider your objection to be both illogical and unreasonable,' a shocked judge complained.

Gilbert was adamant. 'On the contrary, sir, it is neither of those things.

Have you any concept of the suffering notification of a delay would cause Hank Paltroe?'

'Then we won't tell him,' the judge, ready to reach a compromise, replied.

'That would be even more inhumane, Judge.'

'The alternative is a slaughter in Tularosa,' Judge Keily said wearily. 'Will your conscience permit that, Gilbert?'

Turning his head to speak over his shoulder as he headed for the door, Gilbert said, 'My mission is to ensure that the condemned ones suffer as little as possible in their final minutes on earth, Judge Keily. I will afford Hank Paltroe the same consideration as I have all the others. The situation that the town presently finds itself in is, with the greatest respect, Judge, a matter for your conscience, not for mine.'

'Gilbert . . . ' the judge began to plead in desperation.

But the hangman had already left the office.

'This isn't right,' Cora Caddo argued. 'Even if I can help you up into the saddle, there is no way you'll be able to stay there in your condition.'

'Just push,' Clancy said hoarsely, annoyed at his own weakness.

'You should be in bed,' Cora scolded, as she helped him to scramble up so that he was in the saddle, clutching the horn with both hands to steady himself. She ran round the horse to guide his foot into the stirrup.

At Clancy's bidding, but under protest throughout, Cora had borrowed two horses from her friend at the livery. She had brought them round to the rear of the hotel, but even with her assistance, getting Clancy dressed and down the stairs had been a struggle. Cora had regarded buckling on his gunbelt as the most unnecessary of their tasks, but Clancy thought otherwise, and had insisted. Now unable to remember how many times he had blacked out from intense pain along the way, he sat precariously in the saddle. He felt so ill now that even he doubted the wisdom in undertaking what he had in mind.

The whole exercise seemed stupid to Cora, but Clancy knew that it was essential. On learning that Gilbert had refused Judge Keily's request to delay hanging Hank Paltroe, Clancy had known that it was vital that he be in at least some kind of fighting order by morning. He had to be around to implement the plan he had outlined to Josie Paltroe. It was the only way for Hank Paltroe to escape without endangering the lives of anyone in Tularosa. He would play it the way the cards were dealt, but the Paltroe brothers were not of prime importance to him now. Whatever happened, the safety of Madge Keily was Clancy's priority. Her position in the bank put her in the line of fire. Once Hank was out of town, Clancy intended to prevent the raid on the bank from happening, even if it meant putting his life on the line. Knowing Josie Paltroe was enough to convince Clancy that he would be putting his life at risk.

All of which meant that Clancy had to force himself through the pain barrier to become the top gunfighter he had been before his physically damaging confrontation with Tularosa's blacksmith.

As Cora mounted a buckskin gelding, Clancy pointed at her saddle-bags and asked, 'You sure you've got the boxes of shells, Cora?'

Jabbing the flanks of her horse to move off Cora complained, 'I really care for you, Marshal, but you're an ornery cuss where worrying is concerned.'

'It's my nature,' Clancy joked, but couldn't manage a grin because the movement of the horse under him was sending jagged spasms of agony through his body. The most pain was in the left side of his chest where the ends of recently broken ribs were jabbing into him.

With Cora leading the way, they followed a trail through cottonwoods and willows and green little vegas that lead into the mouths of intersecting ravines that relieved the monotony of the grey-brown hills. They rode up the easy slope of an arroyo for about a mile, then Cora turned to the east and they entered a wide canyon.

'Will this suit you, Marshal?' she asked, reining up.

Looking around him, Clancy nodded, 'This will do just fine, Cora.'

Dismounting swiftly, she was hurrying toward him, ready to help him down from the saddle, but Clancy waved her away.

'This is where I have to start doing things for myself, Cora,' he told her, freeing one foot from the stirrup, and putting all of his weight on the other foot to bring his leg over the back of his horse.

Pleased with how well the movement had worked, he was lowering himself to the ground carefully, still with one foot in the stirrup, when pain plunged through his chest like he'd been stabbed with a long-bladed dagger.

Instantly losing his strength, he dropped. Leg twisting painfully before it freed itself from the stirrup, he fell on to his hands and knees, his chest causing so much agony that he was unable to draw a breath.

Running to crouch by his side, Cora held his shoulders but wisely didn't attempt to help him up. Seeing the sweat dripping from his forehead, she chastised herself, 'This is plumb loco. It was his idea, but if he can't make it back into town, then I'll be to blame for making it possible for him to ride out here.'

But Clancy was gradually recovering, and was signalling with jerks of his head for her to help him to his feet. It caused him great pain when, clinging on to Cora, he was at last standing upright. Leaning his back against his horse, gasping for breath, he said, 'I'll be fine, Cora.'

'You are far from fine, Marshal,' Cora rebuked him, adding sternly, 'I'm taking you back to town as soon as you are able to get back on that horse.'

He pleaded. 'No. I'll be fine. Just give me a minute.'

'It'll take more than a minute,' she worriedly predicted.

Cora was right. More than ten minutes went by before a resolute Clancy was able to walk unsteadily away from his horse. Heading for a clearing, he beckoned for her to follow, saying, 'Bring a box of shells with you.'

He stopped some yards from a circular stone that was about eight inches in diameter. Steadying himself, letting the pain he felt balance out so that it lessened significantly, he went for his gun. To Clancy his draw seemed to be in slow motion, and when he did trigger off the shot he was filled with despair. The bullet ploughed a short, dusty path through the ground several inches to the right of the stone.

It was as he had feared. His once

perfect co-ordination between mind and body had been dislocated both by the beating he had taken and the after-effects from which he still suffered. It was vital that he regained that co-ordination. The only way was through perseverance and continuous gunplay practice.

Reholstering the .45 Colt he paused for only a split second. Drawing again, a shade faster than before in his hopeful estimation, he fired and the bullet dug into the ground closer to the stone. Encouraged, he continued drawing and shooting.

Half an hour later, with Clancy bathed in sweat and Cora's hands aching from breaking open boxes of shells for him to reload, he made a breakthrough. A draw that was equal to his old speed was followed by a shot that hit the stone. A second shot, fired almost simultaneously, split the stone in two.

'Is that it, Marshal?' a weary Cora asked hopefully.

His gun back in its holster, Clancy replied 'Not quite, Cora. I'd like you to help me some more.'

Together they commenced a new routine. On Clancy's instructions, Cora picked up a handful of small stones and threw them into the air one at a time. Drawing and firing at every stone, Clancy replaced his .45 in his holster after every shot. It was a long and arduous task. At first he managed to hit only one in four of the stones Cora tossed in the air. But they kept going until Clancy was able to draw and hit the small targets every time.

'I guess that will do just fine,' a satisfied Clancy at last told Cora, who was nursing an aching arm.

By then it was late afternoon, and Cora made a mock complaint. 'Good. With luck I'll be able to get back to town in time to still keep my job at the saloon.'

'I'm sorry, Cora,' Clancy apologized. He hadn't realized how much time had passed. But when they began to return to their horses he discovered that the exertion had severely depleted his strength. As he walked, his legs felt as if he was wading through mud, and on reaching the horses he was ashamed at having to ask Cora to help him up into the saddle.

On the unselfish insistence of Cora, who knew she would be late for work, they took the ride back to town at a leisurely pace. But even that was too much for Clancy. On dismounting at the rear of the hotel, he slumped to the ground, unconscious.

Cora was trying to revive him when Sadie Forston came hurrying out of the hotel. Carrying a bowl of cold water, Sadie knelt beside the prone Clancy. Dipping a cloth in the water she bathed his forehead, talking to Cora as she carried out her task.

'This man should be resting, recovering,' Sadie exclaimed. 'He has no business riding anywhere, least of all out of town.'

'The marshal is a stubborn man,'

Cora was saying, as Clancy's eyelids flickered and he opened his eyes. 'He is determined to be on the streets tomorrow morning.'

'He'll be lucky to be anywhere tomorrow morning,' Sadie commented, as she and Cora raised Clancy into a sitting position.

'Shall we see if we can get him up on his feet?' Cora suggested.

'Not yet, or we may cause him more damage,' Sadie advised. 'Let's give him a little while to recover.'

'It's just that,' Cora began uncomfortably. 'You see . . . it's just that I have to get these horses back to the livery, and I'm already late for work. I don't want to leave the marshal, but my boss is very strict.'

'I know what a saloon girl has to contend with, Cora, believe me,' Sadie said. 'It's probably safe to get him to his feet now. Shall we give it a try?'

As they eased him upright, Clancy returned fully to consciousness, although he was still physically feeble. He felt the warmth of Sadie Forston's body, and caught the womanly scent of her as Cora helped prop him so that the hotel woman could support him while he walked.

'Are you sure that you can manage?' Cora asked.

'Yes, you hurry along, Cora,' Sadie answered.

Unable to turn to look, Clancy heard the creaking of leather as Cora swung up into the saddle, and the clip clop of the hoofs of two horses as the saloon girl moved away. Then, with his strength rapidly returning, he only needed to lean lightly on Sadie as she assisted him toward the back door of the hotel.

Once inside, he took his arm from around her shoulders, telling her, 'Thanks, Sadie, but I can make it on my own from here on.'

'Nonsense. You'll need me to get you up the stairs. Then I'll fetch Doc Hartley.'

'I don't need the doctor,' Clancy said emphatically.

Reaching for his arm, Sadie was putting it back round her shoulders when a door in front of them opened and Matthew Forston appeared.

'Matthew.' Sadie spoke her husband's name in a way that said she was going to ask for his help with Clancy.

But Forston made no response. After spending a long moment staring at his wife and Clancy, he turned and left them, closing the door behind him.

9

It was an unusual and unsettling morning for Madge Keily. The atmosphere out in the streets was eerily tense at the knowledge that a man was soon to be hanged. But what had a more direct effect on Madge was her work. She found it difficult to adjust to being in the bank while it remained closed, its door bolted and barred. They weren't to open that day on the orders of her father. With US Marshal Lombard still out of action through injury, the judge was sure that the bank would be at risk if or when the Paltroe gang came blazing in to rescue the condemned man who was due to step up on the gallows. As her father had explained to Madge and Norman Spelling, all he had to defend the town with was young Tommy Oakes and a group of cowboys with rifles. The judge said that had

Lombard been around it would have been very different, and the bank could have remained open.

Niggling at Madge was her failure, due to not wanting to add to his worries, to inform her father that a stranger had yesterday paid a second visit to the bank. The same gentlemanly figure she had told the marshal about had returned to make some innocuous enquiry. Probably there was nothing in it, but had she the opportunity to do so she would have told Ronan Lombard that the stranger had returned.

Knowing that it was Will Tarner's feelings for her that was at the root of what had happened to the marshal made Madge feel guilty. This feeling was worsened by the fact that she had been unexpectedly overwhelmed with relief on finding herself free of Will Tarner. Though always doubtful about her relationship with him, she hadn't realized how deeply she had disliked the blacksmith's possessiveness.

Will had fled Tularosa now, and the

consensus was that he would never return. That prospect appealed to Madge, although she admitted to herself that she was perhaps being very unkind. She wondered if she would have felt just as dismissive toward Will Tarner had US Marshal Lombard not ridden into town.

'The execution is scheduled for eleven o'clock, isn't it, Madge?' Norman Spelling asked, ending her spell of meditation.

'Yes.'

'Is Judge Keily of the opinion that the risk to the bank will be over then?'

Having noticed Spelling's nerves rapidly getting the better of him, Madge would have liked to say something to calm him. But that would have been to create a false sense of security, so she gave him the facts. 'According to my father, the gang is just as likely to raid the bank after the hanging as before. He advised that we stay closed all day, Norman.'

'We will bow to the judge's wish,' Spelling said, clutching his right hand with his left to stop his fingers twitching. 'But I must say this is quite a nerve-racking situation, Madge.'

Either the manager's fright was catching, or Madge was beginning to suffer from a dread of her own. Whichever it was, she was becoming increasingly jumpy. She put a sensible solution to Spelling. 'Why don't we secure both the money and the bank, Norman, then take the remainder of the day off? That way we will both be safe.'

'Well,' he said, drawing the word out, tempted by Madge's suggestion. Then fear of his employers overcame his fear of the Paltroe gang. 'We couldn't do that, Madge. The bank wouldn't like it if there was a robbery and we had left the premises unoccupied.'

With a soft sigh, Madge prepared herself for a very long and most probably very eventful day.

★   ★   ★

In the lemon yellow dawn of that day the Paltroe gang squatted on a rocky shelf about fifteen feet above the trail into Tularosa. They were so close to town that as a precautionary measure they had hidden their horses in a narrow ravine behind them. Ike Short, Reb Hawker, Bill Coffey, and Luke Sontag listened intently as Josie Paltroe gave instructions for when they reached town. Hunkering among them, Will Tarner was too ill at ease to concentrate on what the gang leader was saying.

'It was fortunate that I went into Tularosa again yesterday,' Josie said, 'otherwise I wouldn't have known that the bank wouldn't be opening. But that's to our advantage.'

'I don't see how that can be, Josie. Busting into the bank is going to bring the whole town down on our backs,' Ike Short voiced his doubts.

'We don't bust in, Ike,' Josie Paltroe explained patiently. 'This is the way we do it. Bill, Luke, and you, Tarner, go into Tularosa first. On the outskirts of town you'll come to some disused stables that were used by the stage before they moved to new premises further in town. You and Luke dismount there, Bill, and hide your ponies in the old stables. Both of you go on foot then, making your way behind the buildings. When you reach the rear of the bank you'll find there's an alley running along the top end of the building. Go down the alley to the street end and stay there, keeping yourselves concealed.

'You, Tarner, ride on up to the bank, nice and slow. When you get there, knock on the door and identify yourself. Make up some tale about wanting to be there to protect the girl and look after the bank. Because they know you they'll open the door to let you in. That's when Bill and Luke go in fast behind you. You two secure the door again and wait till you hear from me. I don't want no shooting, d'you hear? Any problems, you use your knife, Bill.'

'The girl ain't got to be harmed,' Will Tarner's face had gone white. 'Unless you can promise me that, I ain't going along.'

'Two things, Tarner,' Paltroe said quietly but nastily. 'The girl won't come to no harm if she behaves, and you don't have a choice whether or not you goes with us.'

'That's the bank taken care of,' Reb Hawker spoke for the first time. 'How do we get to the jail without getting blasted out of our saddles?'

Paltroe took delight in revealing the cleverest part of his plan. 'Us three only go a little way into town to a yard where a grain merchant keeps his wagons. At that time of the morning at least two of the wagons will have horses harnessed ready to make deliveries. I'll get up on the seat while you and Ike hide yourselves in the bed of the wagon, Reb. That way we'll reach the jail without anyone noticing anything out of the ordinary.'

'Dang me if that ain't one real masterly plan, Josie,' an excited Ike Short congratulated his leader.

'You all can still vote to go along with Clancy's plan if you want,' a pleased Josie said smugly.

'No, no, Josie,' Ike shook his head animatedly. 'Yours sure is a fine plan.'

'Mighty fine,' Hawker agreed.

★   ★   ★

After checking that each and every one of his riflemen was in place in the upper windows of the street, Judge Keily joined up with Tommy Oakes close to the Rest and Welcome Hotel. The deputy town marshal held his rifle across his chest, ready for action. It was just after nine o'clock, with two hours to go before Hank Paltroe was hanged. The townsfolk were going about their business, but in a subdued and cautious manner. The schoolhouse that stood not far from the jail was noticeably quiet and deserted. To the delight of the children of Tularosa, Judge Keily had cancelled lessons for that day.

'You going to check on the marshal,

Judge?' Oakes tried to suppress a grin as he enquired. 'Cora saw him yesterday and said he's still in a bad way.'

The judge nodded. 'As I expected. We are on our own, Oakes.'

Judge Keily was far from being as confident as he appeared to be. Though the bravery of his band of men was admirable, he never lost sight of the fact that he was about to face experienced, resourceful, and professional outlaws with a bunch of enthusiastic amateurs. Any chance of success lay in the outlaw gang approaching the jail by the direct route up the main street. The judge was confident that there was no other way to reach the jail, but it was probable that his local knowledge was no match for Paltroe's ingenuity. Posting a lookout would serve no purpose, as the trail close to town bent round a concealing rocky point, and was then hidden further by a screen of cottonwoods and willows.

The judge told Oakes, 'Our priority must be the jail.'

'It worries me that the reason Hank Paltroe came to town was to size up the place for a bank raid the gang was planning.'

'I haven't forgotten that fact, Oakes,' Keily said, his brow furrowing into a frown. 'I have taken the precaution of having the bank kept securely closed. My hope is that Paltroe will today concentrate on saving his brother from the gallows, and ignore the bank. However, just in case, we'll both go to guard the executioner at the jail now, and one of us can go take a look at the bank later.'

Glancing around him, Tommy Oakes was disturbed. The few people on the streets were too much like ghost figures for his liking. No one seemed to have any interest in anything except to get through that traumatic day peaceably and unharmed. He tried to share that optimism, but knew that Tularosa faced its most testing time ever. It had surprised him to discover that his run-in with the man posing as a US marshal had wrought a change in him. It had instantly turned Tommy Oakes the boy into a man.

But he was a man who, providing he survived the next few hours, would again call out the impostor who had to all intents and purposes stolen his girl. Cora was now more than ever besotted with the stranger.

First things first though, and Oakes put an idea to Keily. 'I was thinking, Judge, that the hanging should be brought forward. If the hangman strings up the prisoner right now, then the gang would have no purpose in coming to town.'

'That occurred to me, Oakes, but the executioner won't budge from the set time of eleven o'clock.'

'But the town's paying him, Judge,' Oakes protested, 'so surely the hangman should do as he's told?'

Uncomfortable at Oakes's logic, the judge answered, 'Gilbert is no ordinary hangman, Tommy, he is an idealist. He has a set programme to which he will

212

brook no alteration.'

'That sure makes it difficult for us, Judge.'

'That is appreciated,' Keily acknowledged. 'Nothing is how I wanted it to be today. I was relying on US Marshal Lombard being in charge.'

'We'll manage without him, Judge.'

Judge Keily could neither share Oakes's dislike of the US marshal nor his contention that they would succeed today without him.

★ ★ ★

Fastening the broad brass buckle of his cartridge belt, Clancy walked out of his room and down the hotel stairs. Pleased at how good he felt, he passed through the entrance hall, aware that Sadie Forston was behind the desk but not looking in her direction. After helping him up to his room the previous evening, an unhappy Sadie had confided that she was planning to leave both her husband and Tularosa. 'I'd welcome the chance to ride out with you when you go, Marshal,' she had told him. 'That's all I'm asking, just to have you help me leave. I'll go my own way after we're clear of Tularosa.' Not believing that he would be able to free himself of her that easily, Clancy had said nothing. Offended, Sadie had been weeping silently when she left his room.

'Marshal . . . ?' she called now as she saw him passing.

Ignoring her, Clancy walked out into the bright morning sunlight. Pausing outside the door, he saw the backs of Judge Keily and Tommy Oakes in the distance. They were heading for the jail. At the sight of them, Clancy felt relief at his sudden and complete recovery: for the judge and young deputy town marshal to take on Josie Paltroe was suicidal.

Turning in the opposite direction to the jail, Clancy made his way to the Majestic Saloon. The yellow cur that was sleeping outside stirred then stood up, stretched and followed Clancy inside. The place was dark and seemingly empty, but Clancy caught a glimpse of a coloured frock at the far end of the bar and knew that it was Cora. That explained why the dog had followed him inside. Aware that Cora was alone, the animal was ready to protect her.

'Ronan!' she exclaimed, coming toward him at a little run. 'What are you doing up and about? You were so ill yesterday that I was awake worrying about you all night.'

'I'm fit again now, Cora. I have work to do, or there will be slaughter on the streets of Tularosa. I've come to ask a favour of you.'

She spread both hands expressively. 'Just ask, and I'll do whatever it is.'

'It could be dangerous.'

'I live a dangerous life, Ronan,' she informed him, with a tight little smile. 'What is it that you want?'

'A horse, saddled and left hitched at the back of the jail.'

'I can do that, Ronan.'

'The timing is important,' Clancy said tersely. 'I want you to deliver the horse there a few minutes before eleven o'clock this morning, then you must get away from that area as fast as you can. Will you promise me that you will do that, Cora?'

A little hurt, she pouted. 'I thought that by now you would know that you can rely on me, Ronan.'

'You've got me wrong.' He smiled tenderly at her. 'I know that you'll have the horse there. What I was asking for was your promise that you will hurry away once you've left it behind the jail.'

'I promise.'

'Thank you,' he said, turning and walking away toward the door.

'Ronan.'

Stopping as she called his name, he turned. 'Yes?'

'When whatever is about to happen is over, would I be right in thinking that you'll be leaving town?'

'That's likely.'

'I suppose it would shame you to

216

take a saloon girl with you?'

Her dark eyes were glinting with unshed tears, and Clancy assured her, 'I don't see you as a saloon girl. To me you are someone very special named Cora.'

'Does that mean a yes?' she asked poignantly.

'Right now it can only mean perhaps. I'm sorry, Cora.'

He walked away and the yellow cur accompanied him off the premises.

On his way to the jail, the heel of Clancy's boot caught against the edge of a slightly raised plank in the boardwalk outside of the two Miss Stewarts' haberdashery store. What should have been an inconsequential half-trip became a disaster for Clancy. A jarring of sensitive nerves passed up through his leg to reawaken the intense pain caused by his fractured ribs. Clutching his side, he staggered and would have fallen if his shoulder hadn't come to rest against the door jamb of the store. Resting for a few moments, taking shallow breaths to avoid raising the level of pain in his chest, Clancy was sorely disappointed to find that he had overestimated his recovery.

Relieved that the agony was easing, he used his shoulder to push him upright. He had taken just one step when pain hit him again, harder this time. So hard that he blacked out, falling sideways to crash heavily against the door. The door gave way and he fell into the store to collapse on to the floor.

★ ★ ★

'Who is it?'

There was a tremor in the voice of Norman Spelling as he responded to the loud banging of the bank door. Madge was trembling a little as she waited for whoever it was outside to reply. They were safe with the door barred and the window shuttered, but with the whole town in a state of high tension, having someone either thumping or kicking the door was frightening.

'It's me, Mr Spelling, Will Tarner. I'm here to help.'

Undecided for a moment, Spelling then drew the bolts on the door and lifted the bar. He was knocked off balance as the door burst open violently. A shocked Madge saw Will Tarner, his damaged face barely recognizable, pushed into the bank by two men who came in behind him. One of them was dark-skinned and with the black eyes and high cheekbones of an Indian. The other man was white, squat, fat and ugly. Both had drawn six-guns in their right hands.

Once inside the bank, they turned and slammed the door shut, bolting and barring it before turning and gesturing for Madge and Spelling to stand close together behind the counter. The ugly fat man spat out an order. 'Stay there where we can see you. If you don't try anything smart, nothing will happen to you. All of us need to wait now, so let's keep it friendly like. You, Tarner, get round there behind the counter with them.'

Unable to understand what Will was doing there, Madge was relieved to learn that at least he didn't appear to be a part of the outlaw gang. Tarner came round the counter and stood between her and Norman Spelling. Holstering their guns, the two outlaws went to the window, faces pressed against the wooden shutter, peering out through slits left on each side of the badly fitting shutter.

Madge felt the back of Will's hand urgently pressing against her thigh. Looking down, she saw his index finger pointing downwards to the floor under the counter. Seeing the double-barrelled shotgun that was kept for emergencies but had never been used, she understood what Tarner wanted. The weapon was within reach of her left foot.

Stretching out her leg, keeping a wary eye on the two outlaws and careful to make no noise, she edged the shotgun toward the blacksmith. It was a slow process, and she had to take a frustratingly long break when the squat outlaw turned away from the window to check on them. For a moment it seemed that he was about to walk over to the counter. But he changed his mind and returned to peer out through the shutters once more. Though she was thankful that they didn't keep a gun on their three prisoners, Madge couldn't understand why they didn't.

Resuming the hooking movement with her foot, she manoeuvred the shotgun so that it lay at Will Tarner's feet. She heard the blacksmith's deep intake of breath, and then he bent quickly to grasp the scattergun. Tarner was upright again, bringing both barrels to bear on the two outlaws, when the man Madge took to be at least part Indian turned to face them.

To Madge all movement seemed to be momentarily slowed. Willing Tarner to pull the trigger, praying for Tarner to pull the trigger, she saw the dark-visaged man's hand go up to the back of his neck.

Then everything came back to a

normal speed. There was obviously a sheathed knife positioned high between the Indian's shoulders. All in one smooth movement that was blurred by speed, he pulled the knife and threw it.

Beside Madge, Tarner made a little sound like a public orator clearing his throat before making a speech. Bemused by the soundless, swift passage of the knife, she hadn't grasped what had happened until the sound of the heavy shotgun hitting the floor focused her mind. Then she saw that a horrified Norman Spelling was holding Tarner with both arrns, trying to hold him up as he started to fall.

Madge cringed at the sight of the bloody pointed end of the knife blade protruding from the side of Tarner's neck nearest to her. Spelling lacked the strength to hold the giant blacksmith and, as Tarner slowly sagged, Madge could see the short handle of the knife on the far side of his neck. There was little blood, but it was obvious that the knife had passed right through the blacksmith's neck.

Madge screamed.

The dark outlaw vaulted over the desk, silenced Madge by hitting her across the mouth with the flat of his hand, and then bent to yank the knife from Tarner's neck. Opening a ledger that was on a small table, the outlaw put the blade in and closed the ledger. When he withdrew the knife the blade was clean and he leapt back over the counter.

Blood gushed from Tarner's throat now the knife had been withdrawn, and he lay on the floor violently convulsing. Having to move to avoid the blacksmith's kicking feet, Norman Spelling cried out as he slipped on the blood and fell. Turning away, Madge bent over and was sick over and over again.

When she turned back, Spelling was standing, his body trembling and his suit and shirt soaked with blood. The fat outlaw was covering them with a six-shooter; Will Tarner had died.

★ ★ ★

A Stewart sister stood on each side of Clancy as he lay on the floor of their shop. Hilda's mouth was moving like she was speaking silently, while a just as alarmed Emily stood doing invisible knitting with trembling fingers.

'He's not dead,' Hilda announced, pointing to the erratic rise and fall of Clancy's chest.

'He may well be if we don't do something,' her sister said, in a hoarse whisper. 'What can we do?'

'Fetch the brandy from the cabinet, Hilda,' Emily ordered. 'That should revive him.'

Turning to obey, Hilda stopped to ask, 'What if either of us are sick and need the brandy when winter comes, Emily?'

'What sort of a Christian are you, Hilda?' Emily scolded her sister, who hurried off to get the brandy.

When she returned Clancy had recovered sufficiently to prop himself up on one elbow. Hilda passed a glass of brandy to Emily, who stayed at arm's length from Clancy when she passed it to him. Taking the glass with a barely audible 'Thank you', Clancy emptied it. Then able to sit up, he reached out a hand for help, first to Emily and then to Hilda. But both spinsters shrank from touching a man.

Having a sudden thought, Hilda brought a dressmaker's dummy over from a corner of the shop and pushed it close to Clancy. At first not understanding, Clancy then clutched at the dummy hand over hand to pull himself to his feet.

With one arm round the dummy and holding his chest with the other hand, Clancy said, 'Thank you, ladies. You are very kind.'

'More brandy?' Emily suggested.

Before Clancy could reply, Hilda cancelled the offer, shaking her head angrily at her sister for making the offer. Using a foot to push a chair across the floor to where Clancy stood, Hilda told him, 'Sit down and get your strength back before you leave.'

10

As Clancy stepped out of the door to join Gilbert as he passed by, the hangman looked with surprise at the haberdashery store and remarked, 'You certainly seem to have an effect on the ladies of Tularosa, Mr Clancy.'

'Not the right sort of effect on those two,' Clancy smiled. Wanting to continue his recovery before the action began, he placed a hand on the hangman's shoulder as they walked. Gilbert shifted the little black satchel he was carrying to his other arm. 'I need to lean on you a little, Gilbert. Let's make this look like two good friends taking a stroll.'

'We are good friends, Mr Clancy, and for selfish reasons I am delighted to have you at my side this morning,' Gilbert said. 'But your state of health is of great concern to me. Are you sure that you are equal to whatever task may lie ahead?'

'I'll handle it,' Clancy answered.

The loyal Cora was passing in the opposite direction on the far side of the street. Knowing that she would have done what he had asked of her, he hated the fact that he was about to badly let down Cora and others who had helped in this town. But his future could lie only with the Paltroe gang. He couldn't stay in Tularosa as Barton Clancy because he was known here as US Marshal Ronan Lombard. That pretence couldn't be continued indefinitely.

'Forgive me should I sound unduly critical, Mr Clancy,' Gilbert began, in his verbose manner, 'but I have my doubts that you can handle what will almost certainly prove to be a violent confrontation, when you need my support to take a simple walk down the street.'

'It's not serious, Gilbert. Some of my ribs have been broken loose and they cause me a problem at times.'

'Then we most hope that it doesn't happen at a wrong time,' Gilbert said, as they stopped outside of the jail and he tapped on the door with his knuckles.

Tommy Oakes opened the door slowly and cautiously, his rifle held at the ready. He showed surprise at seeing Clancy, and a smiling Judge Keily came forward to greet them.

'Gilbert, we are ready for you,' the judge said, before reaching for Clancy's hand and shaking it. 'I can't find the words to tell you what it means to me to have you here with us, Marshal Lombard. But your depleted state of health concerns me.'

'Don't worry about me, Judge,' Clancy said. 'What's the situation at the bank?'

'All's quiet down there, Marshal. Oakes checked it out a little while ago.'

'Is your daughter there?' Clancy asked anxiously.

The judge nodded. 'She is, but the

building is securely barred, bolted and shuttered.'

Still unsure about Madge's safety, Clancy watched Gilbert clasp his little black satchel to him. The hangman then addressed the judge. 'I will go to the condemned one's cell now, Judge Keily. I take it that no clergyman will be in attendance?'

'The prisoner declined Preacher Willard's offer to be with him,' the judge replied.

'I see. Then it is important to minimize Mr Paltroe's distress, so speed is of the essence, although I will never sacrifice either thoroughness or efficiency. It is essential that the doomed one is fully prepared for the last event of his life. If you could have Mr Oakes open the door to the yard ready for the procession to the gallows, which must proceed with dignity and solemnity.' He spoke to Clancy then. 'I would like you to accompany me, Marshal.'

The sound of turning wagon wheels

outside had them all exchange worried glances. The judge signalled to Oakes, who hurried to the window to look out. He turned a smiling face back to Keily. 'It's all right, Judge. Just one of Wally Schonfield's carts on a delivery round.'

—'Life must go on, I suppose,' the judge said philosophically.

When Clancy and Gilbert entered his cell, Hank Paltroe turned from where he had been standing at the window. The outlaw looked past the hangman to Clancy, his eyes silently seeking reassurance. As much as it was possible to communicate in that way, Clancy did his best to convey to Paltroe that everything had been arranged for him to escape.

Intoning sympathetic words too low for Clancy to catch. Gilbert worked fast. Taking from his little black satchel a neatly worked noose he slipped it over the head of Paltroe with such dexterity as to be hardly noticed by the outlaw. Next from the little black satchel there appeared a black hood, and Gilbert had it over the head of the prisoner and Paltroe's arms were pinioned behind his back in a trice.

Standing back to allow the hangman and his captive to pass, Clancy acknowledged that Gilbert had every right to boast about his expertise.

★　★　★

Entering the wagon yard unseen, Josie Paltroe, Reb Hawker, and Ike Short hid behind a stack of fodder close to where a team of horses stood hitched to a cart loaded with sacks of grain. On the far side of the cart, voices came through the open door of a shed.

'Remember,' Paltroe whispered to his men, 'no shooting. Clancy will take the sound of shots as our signal for him to put his plan into action. We don't want that to happen.'

An elderly man came from the shed and waddled on bowed legs to the cart. He was climbing stiffly up to the seat when Paltroe ran swiftly up behind him. Holding his six-gun by the barrel, the outlaw clubbed the old man, crushing the back of his skull.

With an elbow, Paltroe knocked the corpse out of his way and swung up on the seat of the cart. Hawker and Short clambered up on the sacks of grain. With a slap of the reins, Paltroe set the team off fast just as a young man came to the door of the shed, aiming a shotgun at them.

Pulling the horses round fast in an arc so that the cart would pass dangerously close to the shed, Paltroe yelled, 'Finish him!'

Kneeling on the sacks of grain, Reb Walker swung his rifle like a scythe. The butt, given immense power by the rate at which the cart was travelling, caught the man on the side of the head.

Having to duck to avoid the shotgun as it came flying through the air, a laughing Ike Short called back to Paltroe, 'Reb took that *homhre*'s head clean off, Josie.'

If he heard, Paltroe didn't respond as

he concentrated in sending the team out into the street and swinging it to the right. Skilfully steering a zigzag course between buildings, he reined up behind the bank. Stopping his two men from moving sacks to conceal themselves, he said, 'A change of plan, boys. Me and Reb are getting off here. You take the cart on up to the jail, Ike. Tell the judge to let brother Hank go, else we'll deliver his daughter to him butchered like a yearling calf.'

'What about Clancy?' Short asked apprehensively.

Paltroe chuckled. 'Barton Clancy won't cause you no bother when he knows we've got the girl. He's weak like, like those knights in England I read about once. They treat women real good. It's what they call calvary.'

'Chivalry.' Ike Short smiled.

Offended at being corrected, Paltroe asked, 'How come you knows that, *amigo*?'

'I got me educated some as a kid, Josie.'

'That ain't going to be any use to you now,' Paltroe muttered. 'Get yourself up on this seat and get to the jail mighty fast. In a few minutes' time they'll be stringing up Hank.'

★ ★ ★

The stained-brown dial of the jail clock showed that it was three minutes to eleven as Clancy came up the passage-way from the cells. Ahead of him, Gilbert had his hands on the shoulders of the hooded Hank Paltroe, guiding him. Clancy was perturbed at there having been no diversionary gunfire as he had arranged.

'Please form an orderly procession behind me, Judge Keily,' the hangman said. 'I would ask all of you to maintain a sense of occasion, no laughter, no ribaldry. In fact, I would prefer it if no one spoke at all.'

Before Clancy had stepped out of the passageway, the street door opened and a smiling Ike Short stepped in with a

234

friendly, 'Hello, folks.'

Short raised both of his empty hands, palm outwards, as Tommy Oakes brought up his rifle.

'Now then, *muy amigo*,' Short smiled, 'gunplay ain't what's needed here.' His smile broadened as he pointed at the judge. 'I guess you're Judge Keily. Josie Paltroe says if you bring his brother down to the bank unharmed, you can take your daughter home and nobody gets hurt.'

His face ashen, Keily could only gasp, 'Good God!'

Short pointed his finger again, this time at Oakes. 'Take that hood and the rope offen Hank, boy.'

'I must protest in the strongest of terms,' Gilbert said angrily, holding on tightly to Hank Paltroe's shoulders.

'Protest away,' Ike Short invited. 'The longer you does your protesting, the more a knifeman called Luke Coffey will be carving up that pretty girl down at the bank.'

The judge snapped out orders. 'Leave

it, Gilbert. Free the prisoner, Oakes.'

Walking slowly and silently backwards down the passageway, Clancy then turned and ran for the back door. Going out, he unhitched the horse, a small buckskin with an arched neck and legs as trim as those of an antelope that Cora had tied there. Up in the saddle, thankfully free of pain, Clancy took an indirect route to the bank.

Reaching the street, he rode out slowly. Keeping close to the buildings on the same side as the bank, he moved the horse at a walking pace. Nearing the bank his keen eyes scanned the building. Shards of glittering glass littered the rickety broad sidewalk outside the bank. The men inside had taken down the shutter and smashed the glass. That meant that their guns would be covering the street.

Clancy quickly devised a strategy. Forming a corner of the street at the far side of the bank was a ramshackle building. Obviously vacant, a sign fixed only at one end and hanging at an angle over an unglazed window read *The Tularosa Herald*.

If he could make it to that building, Clancy would be at too sharp an angle for the guns in the bank to be a threat, and in an ideal position to negotiate with Josie Paltroe.

Keeping in tight to the edge of the street, where the thick dust muffled the buckskin's hoofs, he approached the bank very slowly. Sure that he could take the men inside by surprise and gallop past the building, Clancy dug the spurs in hard when he was within yards of the bank.

But Reb Hawker stepped from the entrance to an alley and fanned the hammer of his .45. The shot hit the buckskin. Clearing his feet from the stirrups, Clancy slid over the neck and head of the horse as it went down. Hitting the ground at a run, feeling no ill effects from the athletics, he drew his gun. A bullet from Hawker went wide, and he pitched forward as Clancy's shot punched a black hole in the centre of his forehead.

Standing in the street, Clancy came under heavy fire from the bank. Crouched double, he ran for the only cover available — an old log water trough across the street from the bank. Lead sang and whistled in the air around him.

Convinced that he didn't have a chance, Clancy was relieved when he was close enough to throw himself behind the trough. But everything went wrong as he did so. His chest collided with a corner of the water trough, and he hit the ground paralysed by pain.

Hearing Josie Paltroe ask, 'Did you get him, Bill?' Clancy could tell that the gang leader was outside the bank, most probably in the mouth of an alley similar to the one Reb Hawker had stepped out of.

'I think so,' Bill Sontag called from inside the bank.

'Clancy's tricky, so I'm not taking any chances,' Paltroe said. 'Hold everything. There's somebody coming down the street. He's carrying a white flag. They're surrendering, Bill.'

'Who's surrendering?' Luke Coffey called from the bank.

Josie Paltroe confessed his ignorance, 'Beats me, Luke.'

Lying on his back, Clancy discovered he could move his neck a little. By shifting his eyes to the corners he could see up the main street to the jail. Blood freezing in his veins, he saw the high-shouldered figure of Gilbert approaching, holding a white handkerchief on high.

'I am unarmed,' the hangman called to the outlaws. 'There is no need for further shooting. I have a message from Judge Keily. If you send his daughter up the street toward the jail, he will release your man.'

'The judge ain't in no position to give orders,' Josie Paltroe called derisively. 'Who are you, little man?'

Gilbert answered in his polite style, 'You will have heard of me, sir. Back East I am better known as Monsieur New York, but out here in the West I am Gilbert — '

'The hangman!' Paltroe croaked

angrily, as he fired his rifle.

Seeing Gilbert hit, spinning half round before collapsing in the dirt, a cold rage had Clancy ignore his pain. With his body in working order, he drew his gun and raised himself up. Josie Paltroe was standing just yards away, his rifle held in one hand at his thigh as he frowned in puzzlement at something that was occurring up by the jail. Arm resting on the trough, Clancy had taken aim at Paltroe's heart when the outlaw saw him.

Knowing that he could never bring the rifle up in time to save his life, Paltroe was wide-eyed with terror. Any loyalty Clancy owed to the gang leader was cancelled out by the shooting of the unarmed Gilbert, and he tightened his finger on the trigger. The pain knifed through his chest again, unexpectedly and suddenly.

His fingers opened involuntarily to release the .45, which fell into the dust. Defeated by the agony that filled him, Clancy's body flopped across the trough. Once more unable to move, he saw the fear leave Paltroe's face as he brought his rifle up, his eyes bright with killing lust as he looked at Clancy.

Then Clancy heard a loud rumbling behind him and realized that Paltroe had been distracted by the noise. With his limbs gradually and painfully obeying him once again, Clancy dropped down to safety behind the trough. Sitting in the dust, his back propped against it, he looked up the street in amazement.

A team of horses was coming down the street at a gallop, pulling a cart loaded with sacks of grain. Standing up on the cart like a circus performer, reins in one hand and blasting away with a rifle held in his other hand, was Deputy Town Marshal Tommy Oakes.

Guessing that Josie Paltroe had run, Clancy could hear rapid fire aimed at Oakes from the bank as he continued his crazy charge. Fearing that the boy had been hit as he saw the cart veer violently, Clancy raised his arms to protect himself as the swerving cart overturned and sacks of grain spilled in all directions.

Jumping from the springboard, an uninjured Oakes, clutching his rifle, landed on his feet beside Clancy and dropped behind the trough to crouch with him.

Freeing himself from the weight of a sack of grain, Clancy complained laconically, 'That was a dangerous stunt. You could have hurt me.'

'Paltroe was ready to do worse than hurt you,' Oakes grinned. 'Are you all right?'

'I got bad pain, but it comes and goes.'

'Gilbert told me about it,' Oakes said, looking to where Gilbert lay unmoving in the street. 'That's why I came to help.'

'I guess I had you all wrong, Tommy.'

'And me you,' Oakes admitted. 'I reckon as how when this is over we might shake each other by the hand.'

'I wouldn't go so far as to say that,' Clancy said.

Chuckling at that, Oakes told Clancy, 'The judge is in control at the jail. I had the hood and noose off Paltroe, but hadn't freed his arms when the judge took care of that outlaw.'

'He did?' Clancy exclaimed. 'That was Ike Short, a mighty tough *bandido*.'

'There ain't many can get the better of Judge Keily. We locked Paltroe back in a cell. What do we do now?'

Moving to test his chest, pleased to experience no real pain, Clancy outlined a plan he had come up with instantly. 'The way I see it, Josie Paltroe is holed up in an alley at the top end of the bank. If you keep them busy, I'll make a run for an opening at the other end of the bank and try to creep up on him. You ready?'

Nodding, Oakes knelt up, levelled his rifle and began firing. Clancy ran, and the outlaws seemed so intent on returning Oakes's fire that they didn't see him go. Jumping over the body of Reb Hawker, he went in through the passage and came out behind the bank. Peering round the corner into the top alley, he saw Paltroe with his back to him, returning Oakes's fire.

Unheard because of the gunfire, Clancy crept up on the outlaw and pressed the barrel of his .45 into his spine. With his mouth close to Paltroe's ear, he said, 'Drop your rifle, Josie, and tell your men in the bank to throw their guns out.'

Paltroe's rifle fell to the round, but he made no attempt to call to his men. Instead, he said in a friendly, coaxing way, 'Come on, Barton, whose side are you on? Me'n you are pardners from way back. We take care of that kid out there, then we can clean out the bank and ride off rich, just like in the old days.'

'Tell your men to throw out their guns,' Clancy repeated.

With a slight shake of his head, Paltroe said, 'I'm not going to do that, Barton, because you won't pull that trigger if I don't. You ain't the type to shoot an old *amigo* in the back.'

'I guess you're right,' Clancy admitted, removing his gun from where it pressed into the outlaw's spine.

Paltroe's soft, short laugh died on his lips as Clancy lowered the muzzle of the gun and shot him in the lower left leg. The bullet nipped through the calf muscle and shattered the bone. Screaming in pain, Paltroe fell sideways as his leg gave out on him. Stopping him from falling, Clancy swung him round and pushed the barrel of his .45 hard into his throat.

'Now shout to your men, Josie.'

In a weak voice, Paltroe shouted, 'Luke, Bill, throw out your guns.'

As the two outlaws obeyed, Tommy Oakes joined Clancy and Paltroe at the back door. A white-faced Norman Spelling opened it. Clancy holstered his gun and stepped to where a shaking Madge was slumped against the counter.

'It's over now, Miss Keily,' he said softly. Seeing the dead Will Tarner on the floor close to her, he took her elbow and moved her away to stand by a wall. 'Gilbert's been shot, and I have to go check on him. I'll be right back.'

The girl nodded numbly. About to go out of the door. Clancy heard Madge's warning cry, 'Ronan!'

Pivoting on his heel, instinctively drawing his gun. Clancy saw the flash of a steel blade thrown by Coffey. Clancy fired, the bullet went deep into Coffey's heart. The knife thudded into the door jamb just inches from Clancy's throat, and was still vibrating as he turned and walked out of the door.

He found Gilbert lying face down. Gently turning him on to his back, Clancy could have cried out in joy as he saw Gilbert's eyes flicker open. 'You're alive, Mr Clancy.'

'And so are you,' Clancy smiled. 'You got plugged in the left shoulder, Gilbert. I'll go get Doc Hartley to fix you up. You've sure got a lot of hanging to do here in Tularosa.'

'Will you be here, Mr Clancy?'

Gilbert asked in a faint voice.

'No, but I hope that we may meet again some day,' Clancy replied, walking hurriedly away.

His final act of deceit in Tularosa would be to claim the US marshal's horse at the livery like it was his own, and ride away. But he was shaken to see Cora Caddo waiting for him. He had made the girl no promise, but that didn't help his conscience.

'Look, it's this way, Cora . . . ' he began, but she stopped him smilingly.

'Don't look so frightened. Marshal,' she gave a soft little laugh. 'I'm here just to tell you that Judge Keily wants to see you at his house. I'll walk with you.'

A stern-faced judge was waiting for them on the veranda, with Tommy Oakes at his side. A hopeful Clancy looked for Madge, but she was nowhere in sight.

'I'm glad to see you,' the judge greeted him. 'This town is indebted to you, Marshal.'

Embarrassed, Clancy looked at the judge, Oakes, and Cora in turn. It wouldn't be possible to live with himself if he didn't confess.

'I've got to be straight with you, Judge. I'm not who you think I am. I used you.'

The judge glared at him fiercely. 'I know who you are, Clancy.'

'How long have you known?' Clancy stammered.

The judge suddenly beamed a wide smile at him, 'Since the day I stopped you when you were riding into town. I could tell you were a fighting man, and that was what Tularosa badly needed. It was me who destroyed the Wanted dodger when young Tommy found it.'

'You're as big a fraud as I am, Judge,' Clancy grinned.

'That's an insult. I'm a much bigger fraud than you are,' Judge Keily laughed. 'Now, I'm offering you the job as town marshal here, permanent. What do you say?'

Wanting to accept, Clancy knew that

he couldn't. 'I'm honoured, Judge, but I've lied to quite a few people, your daughter in particular.'

'I've explained everything to Madge, and she understands. Go in and see her, she's waiting for you in the house.'

'Then I guess you've got yourself a marshal, Judge,' Clancy said, and, as he passed Cora, she whispered to him, 'More good news for you. Sadie Forston left town on the afternoon stage.'

Standing in the doorway, Tommy Oakes held out his right hand and looked at it sorrowfully. 'It'll be real odd being deputy to a man who can't bring himself to shake me by the hand.'

'I'm proud to shake you by the hand, Tommy,' Clancy said.

As he walked eagerly into the house he was pleased to see Cora take the hand he had just shaken into hers.